THE
WHISPERING
HOUSE

THE
WHISPERING
HOUSE

REBECCA WADE

Delta County Libraries

PO BOX 858
Delta, CO 81416
www.deltalibraries.org

KATHERINE TEGEN BOOKS
An Imprint of HarperCollins Publishers

Katherine Tegen Books is an imprint of HarperCollins Publishers.

The Whispering House
Copyright © 2012 by Rebecca Wade

Library of Congress Cataloging-in-Publication Data
Wade, Rebecca.
    The whispering house / Rebecca Wade. — 1st ed.
        p.   cm.
    Summary: When the Price family moves into Cowleigh Lodge while their home is being repaired, fourteen-year-old Hannah discovers that the ghost of a girl who died there at age eleven wants help unraveling the mystery of her 1877 death.
    ISBN 978-0-06-077497-4 (trade bdg.)
    [1. Haunted houses—Fiction. 2. Ghosts—Fiction. 3. Family life—England—Fiction. 4. Dolls—Fiction. 5. Moving, Household—Fiction. 6. England—Fiction. 7. Mystery and detective stories.] I. Title.
PZ7.W118213Whi   2012   2011019975
[Fic]—dc22   CIP
                                                                     AC

Typography by Carla Weise
12 13 14 15 16   CG/RRDH   10 9 8 7 6 5 4 3 2 1
❖
First Edition

FOR TORI

CONTENTS

"Would you like me to read you a story, Angelina? Then sit up straight, like a good girl—don't slouch. There . . . that's better. Now I shall begin.

"There was once a little brother who took his sister by the hand and said, 'Since our own dear mother's death we have not had one happy hour; our stepmother beats us every day and, when we come near her, kicks us away with her foot. Come, let us wander forth into the wide world.' So all day long they traveled over meadows, fields, and stony roads. By the evening they came into a large forest, and laid themselves down in a hollow tree, and went to sleep.

"When they awoke the next morning, the sun had already risen high in the heavens, and its beams made the tree so hot that the little boy said to his sister, 'I am so very thirsty that if I knew where there was a brook, I would go and drink. Ah! I think I hear one running.' And so saying, he got up and took his sister's hand, and they went to look for the brook. The wicked stepmother, however, was a witch, and had witnessed the departure of the two children; so, sneaking after them secretly, as is the habit of witches, she had enchanted all the springs in the forest.

"I think I shall stop reading now, Angelina, for the sun is

making my head ache. I wish the trees did not crowd so close. But if I shut my eyes, I cannot see them. That is better. I will sleep now. You may sleep too if you like."

"Angelina? Are you awake? Please pay attention, for I cannot speak too loudly in case someone hears. Now listen. I have no idea why we have been brought to this wood, but I fear we have been left alone, like those poor children in the other story whose evil stepmother turned them out of their father's house to wander until they lost their way and fell asleep beneath a great tree and were covered with leaves so that they were not found until the spring and they were both quite dead! Or perhaps I am wrong, and soon we shall see a little cottage made of delicious things to eat, but you know, we must not touch anything in case the wicked witch comes out and captures us, for that is what witches do. And we shall know her because she will be most dreadfully ugly—that is another thing about witches, they are always dreadfully ugly—but we must be very quiet, like little mice, and make no sound; then perhaps she will not notice us."

"Angelina, listen to me. This is very serious. We must have fallen asleep again, and while we slept, someone has lit a fire. I can hear it crackling. I expect it was a poor woodcutter who saw us here and took pity on us. He will have made the fire to warm us so that we will not die of cold. But he has lit it altogether too near the trees, which is odd, because a woodcutter should know better than to do such a foolish thing. However, I daresay he will be along presently and see the danger. Then he will draw water from the well and put the fire out and take us to his humble cottage, where his wife will be kind to us and give us bread and milk for supper and put us to bed. Then she will run as fast as her legs can carry her to tell Mama that we are here, and Mama will be very angry with the people who brought us to this forest, and she will rescue us and take us home and hold us close and tell us that never, ever again will she let us out of her sight.

"But hush now. Do you hear a rustling noise? And I believe there is a shape moving in the trees. I cannot see it clearly, but I feel sure that someone is there. It must be the woodcutter, come to rescue us. Yes! I see him now, only it is not the woodcutter, for this person is wearing a long skirt, so perhaps it is the woodcutter's wife. Yes, that must be it. See, she comes nearer, and she is holding a cup. What can be in it, do you suppose? Soon we shall know . . . she is close now. . . .

"Oh! Oh, Angelina! What is happening? The story is all wrong! It is not the woodcutter's wife. . . . It is . . . it is the wicked witch, who has found us after all!"

MISGUIDED MISSILE

It was three o'clock on a Thursday afternoon, and Hannah Price was sitting in the school library wishing there had been no such person as Napoleon Bonaparte. This wasn't because she had anything particularly against the French emperor himself—Hannah was a fair-minded girl—but she couldn't help thinking that it would have been nice if he hadn't chosen to lead quite such a busy, complicated life.

Besides, there were three things getting in the way of her trying to memorize exactly when Napoleon had done what and to whom. The first was that Emily Rhodes, sitting next to her, seemed to have lost something and was searching the table agitatedly; the second, that her friend Sam Fallon was busy perfecting his design for a paper fighter jet and shooting the results in her direction; and the third reason was that it was the last period in the afternoon. She was tired and wanted to go home.

"Must you?" she muttered as the latest model described a graceful arc before glancing off her left ear.

"Sorry," said Sam, in a whisper that could be heard all over the library. "It shouldn't have done that." He picked up the plane and examined it critically, tweaking one of the tail fins before sending it off on a second trial. This time it flew in a more or less straight line past her nose and came to rest behind a radiator. He got up to retrieve it just as the bell rang for the end of school.

"Has either of you seen my notes on the death of Napoleon?" demanded Emily, now that talking was officially allowed.

"Mmm . . . ? Don't think so." Sam made a small adjustment to the fuselage.

Hannah shook her head. "What do they look like?"

"Just a page of typed notes. It must be here somewhere. I had it five minutes ago." Emily sifted once more through the neat pile of notebooks in front of her, looking bewildered. "I just don't understand it. I never lose things!"

"Wait a moment. I may have picked it up by mistake." Hannah began searching her own slightly disordered notes. "No. Sorry, it's not here. Why d'you need it, anyway? Napoleon died in exile, didn't he? We're never going to get asked a question on that."

"Of course not." Emily looked superior. "I was just reading around the subject. I downloaded that page from the internet because it was so interesting."

"Oh?" Hannah began packing away her books, hoping Emily wasn't going to delay her going home by explaining exactly why it was so interesting.

"Fascinating, in fact."

"Okay." Hannah sighed, since Emily was clearly about to tell her anyway. "How *did* Napoleon die?"

"Well, he was in exile, of course, like you said, in a small room in a house on the island of Saint Helena, and he was convinced there was a plot to poison him, you see, but nobody was ever accused at the time. Then, years later, it turned out that a lock of his hair had been kept, and by that time it was possible to analyze it, and it was found to contain traces of arsenic. Except that now they don't think it was the cause of his death, but it could have hastened it by—" She broke off as the jet fighter hurtled toward her from the other end of the library, swiftly followed by its proudly cheering inventor.

Emily glared at it, then at him. "There's no point in continuing this now," she said to Hannah. "I'll tell you later." With a small toss of her gleaming blond head, she strode off.

"What's the matter with her?" inquired Sam, bending to pick up the aircraft and tossing it onto the table while Hannah hurriedly tried to finish packing her own things before they got mixed up with his.

"I think it's just knowing that you two share the same planet upsets her sometimes." She shook her head sadly.

"What was she going on about, anyway?"

"Napoleon. Apparently, toward the end of his life, he thought someone was trying to poison him."

"It's a pity nobody thought of that twenty years earlier. It'd have saved everyone a lot of trouble. Including us."

"Then something else would have happened, and we'd have had a whole lot of different stuff to learn. You never know, it could have been worse."

"Even more boring, you mean? Impossible! History's just a bunch of dead people making stupid mistakes. What's the point in learning about that?"

"So that people who are still alive can avoid making even more stupid mistakes?"

"Huh! You think it's worked?"

"Maybe not yet," she admitted. "I suppose people are still hoping."

If visitors had happened to walk into the library just then and glanced toward Hannah and Sam, they would have seen two perfectly ordinary fourteen-year-olds getting ready to go home from school. They might have noticed that the boy was thin, red haired, with a freckled face and restless, inquisitive eyes. Looking at the girl, they would have seen that she had dry, light-brown hair, a figure prone to puppy fat, and a plumpish face that, though quite pretty when she smiled, when she was anxious (which she frequently was when Sam was around) had the look of a nervous hamster. Rather an unlikely companion for a boy like that, the visitors might have thought. A bit dull, even.

But if those same visitors had happened to see the girl with a pencil in her hand and a sketchbook in front of her, they would have had a surprise. Because as soon as Hannah Price began to draw, she turned into a quite different person. Quick, confident, scarily accurate, she could draw people in a way that made you see things about them you hadn't noticed before.

Sometimes it got her into trouble. Like the time a year and a half ago when it had led to both her and Sam being drawn into a tense search for a tiny wooden statue that had gone missing from the cathedral. By the time it was discovered and returned, a surprising number of people had become involved, including several teachers, an old lady on the school visiting list, two bewildered policemen, and a bishop.

But that had been an exception. Mostly it was Sam who got into trouble, while Hannah did her best to avoid it. And not surprising, most people would say, seeing that Sam's father had, until eighteen months ago, made a dodgy living as a small-time housebreaker specializing in petty theft, whereas Hannah's was a highly respected lecturer in history at the city university. Much more surprising was that they should ever have become best friends in the first place. It was a puzzle.

But if it was a mystery to everyone else, it was one that neither Sam nor Hannah had ever bothered to analyze. They just knew it worked. Even if he did insist on pelting her with wastepaper while she was trying to concentrate on the Battle of Waterloo.

The weather was warm, the sky hazy as they strolled across the playground, out of the school gates, and into Tanners' Lane. From here it was only a short walk to the cathedral square, where they had to go off in different directions, and their pace slowed as they chatted. Then Hannah stopped suddenly and looked overhead.

"What's the matter?" he asked.

"Nothing." She shook her head and started

walking again, faster this time.

Sam quickened his stride to keep up. After a few minutes he glanced sideways at her. "Are you okay?"

"I suppose so."

"Only I can't help noticing you've stopped talking to me."

"What? Sorry. It's just exams coming up. That always makes me edgy."

"Also, it's Friday tomorrow and you still haven't invited me to see your new house."

"Was that a subtle hint that you want to come over?"

"Maybe."

"Okay." They had reached the end of the lane now. She smiled at him. "How about Saturday morning? I'll give you a guided tour."

"Good. About time, too!"

She watched him go. But as soon as he was out of sight, the smile faded. Because it wasn't exams that were making her anxious just then. It was something else. Something she'd seen a moment ago, when she'd happened to look up.

COWLEIGH LODGE

HANNAH HADN'T REALLY MOVED; at least not permanently. It was just that after three very dry summers, the Price family home had "settled." This wasn't nearly as reassuring as it sounded, and had a thoroughly unsettling effect on Hannah and her parents, as it turned out to be a polite way of saying that the house was collapsing. In fact, when the surveyor came to make his report, he shook his head so gloomily and left so hurriedly afterward that Mr. Price understood there was no time to lose and made immediate plans to move his family out.

The house he found was in a quiet residential district about a quarter of a mile from the city center and within easy walking distance of the school. It was on a bus route, with a post office and a small grocery store a few minutes' walk away.

"The rent's pretty low for that neighborhood, isn't it?" Mom frowned thoughtfully. "Why d'you think that is?"

"No idea," said Dad. "What's more important is that it's available straightaway and we can move in as soon as we like. It's only for a few months, after all."

And when they first went to inspect it, there didn't seem to be any problems. The house itself had been built in the 1850s and was of red brick, similar to its neighbors on either side but well detached from them and surrounded by an overgrown garden with a high laurel hedge. The garden was reached by a small iron gate opening onto a paved path, which led unswervingly to a blue front door flanked on either side by ground-floor windows. There were two identical upper-story windows above, and a tiled roof with two chimneys, exactly centered. It looked, thought Hannah, seeing it for the first time, like a child's drawing in its simple symmetry, but at the same time prim and, despite its not-too-distant neighbors, rather lonely. This impression was reinforced rather than dispelled on the inside, where any character the house might once have had was now either removed or covered up by a bland coat of cream paint.

The only slight drawback was that out of the three

bedrooms, one was excluded from the rental agreement owing to storm damage, and was therefore locked. But as Dad pointed out, although the extra space would have been useful for storing things, they really needed only two bedrooms, and in any case, they were getting the house cheaply enough considering the area.

Five days later, on a bright, sunny day in the second week in May, the family moved in. To begin with, there was so much to do, carrying crates and boxes, unloading and stacking books, hanging clothes in the musty-smelling wardrobes and generally trying to make the place feel like home, that Hannah didn't get a chance to consider whether she liked the house or not. It was simply a space into which they somehow had to fit all their possessions, and for a while it seemed less like a house than a rather challenging jig-saw puzzle they were all trying to solve. But gradually Hannah's mother came to terms with the smallness of the kitchen, her father found space for his books and CDs, Toby figured out how to use the cat flap, and the furniture mostly stopped looking like a bunch of uninvited guests at a party and settled itself down.

They had been there about a week when the weather turned close and humid, giving way to a spell of light but persistent rain. That night Hannah had a dream.

She was lying on her back in a wood, surrounded

by bright-green leaves on which the sunlight struck, making them sparkle. The leaves were quite still—the sky between them creamy white, as though faintly overcast—and nearby, birds were singing. Somewhere a fire was lit. She couldn't see it, but she could hear the gentle crackle and snapping of twigs. And she could see a face. A face with a smiling mouth and curious, rather expressionless eyes.

That was all. Nothing happened. There was nothing especially frightening about the dream, and she would have forgotten all about it, except that the following night she had it again. And again the night after that. Each time it was the same.

Then, for no apparent reason, the dreams stopped. The weather cleared, the nights lost their damp clamminess, and she slept soundly. Gradually the memory began to fade.

Until just then, in Tanners' Lane, she had seen something that, for a brief moment, had brought it back. It was an ash tree, in full summer leaf. There should have been no reason why the pattern of leaves against the pale sky filled her with sudden apprehension.

Except that the sky in her dream had been pale, just like that. And the bright-green leaves, she now knew, had been ash leaves.

She shook herself impatiently and went on walking, trying to fill her mind with cheerful thoughts. If she got up reasonably early on Saturday and did some studying before eleven, she could enjoy Sam's visit with a clear conscience. When she'd offered to give him a guided tour of the new house, it had been a joke, of course—there was nothing of interest to see at Cowleigh Lodge—but it might be fun to have someone else to share it with, and if anyone could clear the dusty cobwebs of memory from her brain, it was Sam Fallon.

Her determined optimism took a slight knock when she got home and saw the anxious look on her mother's face.

"What's the matter?"

"Your father's got to go away for a month."

"Where to?"

"America."

"*America?* That's cool! Are we going too?"

"While you're still in school? No chance, I'm afraid. Anyway, he's been offered a lecture tour, so he'll be traveling around a lot. He's standing in for someone who had to cancel suddenly."

"When does he leave?"

"The day after tomorrow. His flight to Washington is at eight a.m."

"Oh!" Hannah perched on a kitchen stool, feeling suddenly deflated. She frowned. "Don't you need visas and stuff to go to the U.S.A.?"

"They fixed him up with an emergency interview. He's known about this for a week, apparently, but didn't want to worry me with it until he knew it was all sorted and he was going for certain." Her mother looked bewildered. "If only he'd told me sooner, I could have helped him get ready, made a list of things for him to bring back. We could have arranged for my aunt to visit him—you know, Aunt Ruth who lives in Philadelphia? But she doesn't do email and I don't have her phone number, so it would have meant a letter, but I know she'd have loved to see him if only I'd had a bit of time to *organize* things."

Hannah turned away to hide a smile. She was fairly certain she knew why her father had made quite sure Mom didn't have too much time to organize anything. Still, it was tough on her. "You're going to miss him. We both are."

"Well, yes, and I wish he didn't have to go away just *now*. What if something were to go wrong? Something the real estate agent hasn't told us about?"

"Don't worry," said Hannah soothingly. "It's only a month. And anyway, nothing's going to go wrong."

THE BOOK

THE NEXT DAY BEGAN clear and bright, but by midmorning the sky had clouded over, and although the temperature remained high, the air had turned humid again. Lessons passed sluggishly; with exams so close, no new work was being given now, and the constant reviewing of topics studied over the past year lent its own staleness to the atmosphere in the classroom.

Standing in the queue for lunch, Hannah noticed a tall, thickset boy sitting at a table on his own. His jutting forehead, flattish nose, and square, prominent chin gave him an aggressive look.

"Who is that?" she asked Sam.

"Dunno," he replied, squinting at the boy. "Never seen him before."

"Do you know who it is, Susie?"

Their friend Susie was standing a couple of places farther up the queue and stood on tiptoe to see where Hannah was pointing. "Uh-uh." She shook her head. "Looks scary, though."

"Well, *someone* must know who he is. And why's he sitting on his own?"

"His name is Bruce Myers, and he's new," said Emily, who had joined the queue late because she'd stayed behind after class to ask the teacher a question, and as usual seemed to know everything.

"Which class is he in?" Hannah looked puzzled. "He looks about our age, but I didn't see him this morning."

"That's because he's in class seven. He's just big for his age. From what I can gather, there was some kind of problem at his last school."

"What kind of problem are we talking about?" Sam narrowed his eyes. "Arson? First-degree murder? The guy looks capable of anything to me."

"Maybe we should go and sit with him," suggested Hannah. But nobody seemed very keen on this idea, and in any case, by the time they had collected their lunch from the counter, the boy had left his table and the four of them took it over. Within five minutes, they had forgotten all about Bruce Myers.

—⋙—

Before going to bed that night, Hannah said good-bye to her father, who would be leaving before she was up the next morning.

"Don't forget to email me," he said, hugging her. "I'll need some news from home to keep me going while I'm out there."

"I won't," she promised.

Earlier in the evening it had begun to rain lightly, and her bedroom felt slightly damp. She undressed quickly and was hanging up her school skirt when she noticed something unusual about the closet. This was a door fitted in front of a recess beside what had once been a fireplace but was now boarded up. The back and sides of the recess had been papered over—several times by the look of it—and the layers had hardened with age and dried mildew to a brittle, boardlike mass that had come away from the original plaster at one side, leaving a gap of about four inches between it and the wall at the top of the recess.

It would be easy to drop something down there, thought Hannah, frowning, but not so easy to get it back again, maybe. Pressing her head against the wall, she peered into the dark little space and saw that somebody had clearly done just that. A rectangular object was wedged about three feet down. She reached her arm into the space and found she could just feel whatever it was, but without being able to get a hold on it. Straightening up, she took a wire coat hanger from the rail and bent it into a roughly square shape, which she lowered into the space until the bottom part of the hanger felt as if it was underneath the obstruction. Then she carefully raised it far enough to be able to grab the object with her hand and bring it into the open.

Coughing, she took her find to the window and brushed away the thick layer of dust and cobwebs to reveal a book. The faded gold lettering showed it to be a volume of illustrated children's fairy tales with stiff covers that had once been red but now were dingy and blotched by the same damp that had attacked its resting place. The pages were hard to separate, and when she pried open the cover, a piece of paper fell out and fluttered to the floor. She bent down to pick it up and laid it on the bed while she examined the book. On the flyleaf was an inscription in ink, faded now to the color of boiled spinach water:

To Maisie.
From your loving papa.
Christmas 1876

On the opposite page, a childish hand had written in pencil:

Maisie Hall. This is her book.

She looked curiously at the looped, slightly uneven letters. Had Maisie slept in this room? And if so, what would she have thought, waking up on that long-ago Christmas morning to find, not this faded, stained old volume, but an exciting new book with pages white and crisp as new linen and shiny scarlet covers with gleaming gold lettering?

But then, she told herself, the book might simply have come from a secondhand shop and been dropped there quite recently. It didn't take long for things to gather dust in an empty house. She put it down on the bedside table and was about to get into bed when she noticed the sheet of paper still lying there. At first she thought it was a page of illustration, come loose from the book, but then she saw that the paper had a different quality altogether and had simply been folded in half to fit inside. Unfolding it revealed a single page torn from a calendar showing the month of June and the year, 1877. Like the book, it was stained and brown spotted, but the days and dates were still perfectly legible. In fact—she glanced at her watch in mild surprise—the page had an odd appropriateness, for today was Friday, the first of the month. And it just so happened that in 1877, June the first had also fallen on a Friday.

For some reason, the page bothered her. Why had somebody decided to tear out this particular month? A calendar wasn't a thing you kept, like a diary. It was simply a useful reminder of things to come, not a record of what had already happened. And in any case, there was nothing written here. That was the trouble.

On an impulse, she reached into her schoolbag for a pencil and her exam timetable and carefully copied the times of all her exams onto the stained, slightly brittle paper. Then she drew a neat line through today's date, tucked the page into the edge of the mirror on the chest of drawers where she would be able to see it each morning, and got into bed. Somehow it felt right that those blank days should be filled in now. At the end of the month, she would throw the page away. After nearly 140 years, it would at last have served its original purpose.

She lay down and went to sleep.

When she woke, it was still dark. The rain was pattering against the windowpane, but the room felt hot and airless and there was a strange smell—vaguely chemical. She sat up, groped for the switch on the bedside lamp, found it, and as the room flooded with light, sank back against the pillows, sweating. It had been the same dream. The wood with the vivid green leaves against the flat, overcast sky, the birds singing, the fire quietly crackling nearby, and the odd, smiling face had all been just as before.

It was only now, on waking, that she obscurely knew it hadn't been a pleasant dream.

THE ATTIC

THE NEXT THING SHE was conscious of was what sounded like the persistent wailing of a young child just below her window. Getting out of bed, she peered out the window to see a grayish, murky daylight with a fine drizzle falling and Toby having a standoff with a rangy-looking ginger tomcat. She glanced at her watch. Eight thirty. So she must have fallen asleep again, eventually.

Hannah showered and dressed, wondering why the house was so quiet, until she remembered that her mother had taken Dad to the airport and wouldn't be back until the afternoon. As she crossed the upstairs landing, her eye fell on the door of the locked bedroom. What was behind that door? Probably four damp walls and a lot of flaking plaster, she told herself firmly.

The dull paintwork had a depressing feel in this light, and she wandered disconsolately downstairs to the pale, tidy kitchen that now smelled faintly of bleach and poured herself a bowl of cereal.

Afterward, she went into the living room to do some studying. Searching in her schoolbag for a text-book, she noticed, with a mixture of amusement and irritation, one of Sam's paper airplanes at the bottom. There was no point throwing it away just now—she'd do a real clear out later, if she had time.

After working steadily for an hour on some geography notes, she felt more cheerful and rewarded herself with a mug of hot chocolate and a couple of cookies, pleased that her mother wasn't there to comment on the probable effect on her waistline.

Now for some biology. She opened the textbook and began to read.

Photosynthesis is the way a plant makes food for itself. Chlorophyll in the green part of the leaves captures energy from the sunlight, which powers the building of food from carbon dioxide and water.

Green leaves. Sunlight. Why that sudden prickle of unease? She stood up and walked to the window. The drizzle was still falling. Sitting down again, she tried to concentrate on work, but the edginess refused to go, making her get up from time to time to wander restlessly around the room.

When the doorbell rang, she almost jumped out of her skin. She froze for a moment, then walked nervously across the hallway and opened the door a couple of inches.

Sam stood on the step.

Hannah opened the door wide, and he walked in, carrying a cellophane-wrapped bunch of purple tulips. "From my mom," he said, holding the flowers at arm's length as if he wanted to get rid of them as soon as possible. "Housewarming present."

"Thanks." Hannah grinned and took the flowers from him.

He glanced speculatively at the mug on the table. "Hot chocolate?"

"Sure. And I'll have some more to keep you company." She resolutely dismissed the image of her mother's outraged stare and led him into the kitchen, where she got the milk out of the refrigerator and put it in a saucepan on the stove, arranging the flowers in a vase while it heated up.

Five minutes later they were back in the living room, the tin of cookies on the table between them, and Hannah wondered why she'd ever been spooked by a biology textbook.

"Nice place." He glanced around him, sipping noisily.

"It's okay. A bit small." Then she felt guilty, remembering the apartment, half the size of this, where Sam lived with his parents and younger brother and sister, who were twins. "We've got too much furniture. And there's no garage or shed. That's why it feels small."

He finished his drink and stood up. "Come on, then. Give me that guided tour."

"Okay. We may as well start with the garden. There's not much to see, but never mind." She opened the French doors at the end of the room and led him down some stone steps onto a small terrace, beyond which was an overgrown lawn surrounded by borders that clearly hadn't been weeded for a long time. Just beyond the terrace, facing the house, was a slatted wooden bench with ornate wrought-iron armrests. Until that moment, Hannah hadn't noticed that it was odd that the bench was facing the house when it would surely have been more natural that it should look out onto the garden. But then, she thought, just now the garden was hardly worth looking at. In any case, Sam showed little interest, so she took him back into the house.

The other room on the ground floor had the same

cream-painted walls and beige carpet as the one they'd been sitting in, and both rooms had high mantel-pieces above what must once have been handsome fireplaces but were now, like the one in Hannah's bed-room, boarded up. In the first room, a modern electric heater stood in the hearth. Here, someone had tried unsuccessfully to liven up the blank board with a vase of dusty dried flowers. In both cases the effect was depressing. Hannah and Sam didn't stay long.

The predictably beige-colored staircase led to a landing with four doors leading off it. Hannah showed him the bathroom, the large room at the front that her parents slept in, and the smaller one at the back, which was hers.

When they came to the fourth door, Sam tried it and frowned. "Why's this one locked?"

"We're not allowed to use it. The real estate agent has the key."

"What's in there?"

"I've no idea. Like I said, we don't have the key."

He looked at her as if she'd said that she was sit-ting in the dark because she couldn't figure out how to use the light switch. "Do you own a screwdriver?"

"I guess so. Dad was using one to fix a hinge on a cupboard last night." She went back down to the kitchen and returned with a toolbox.

Sam ran a professional eye over the assembled contents and selected a small screwdriver.

"What are you going to do?"

"Unscrew the lock, of course."

"But the agent said not to use that room."

"Well, we're not going to use it, are we? We're just going to take a look inside."

"Maybe they have a reason for not wanting us to go in," she said lamely, but she knew when she was beaten, and in any case, Sam had already loosened all four screws and was carefully removing the lock. He laid it on the floor, tipped the screws inside, and pushed open the door.

A first glance told them there was nothing sinister in that room, unless you counted bare floorboards and discolored walls as sinister. In shape it was very like its opposite number on the other side of the landing, the one taken by her parents, except that it was slightly larger and had two windows, not one, which gave it a lighter, more welcoming feel. The smell of mildew was unpleasant, though, and the room felt cold.

"Let's go," Hannah said, shivering. "There's nothing to see in here. The real estate agent was right—it's just storm damaged. I guess the roof has leaked sometime."

"Mmm." Sam ran his hand over a gray-mottled

wall. "This paper looks likes it's as old as the house. You can feel the plaster underneath."

She noticed that the walls had been stripped down, leaving a faint pattern of very pale pink stripes on what would once have been a creamy background, maybe. It was hard to tell in some places, but in others the damage wasn't so bad, and the wall opposite the front window was in fair condition. You could even see the darker squares and rectangles where somebody had once hung pictures. There was something faintly indecent about those marks. It was as though the house, elsewhere so clean and primly covered up, here was revealed in its grubby underwear. She shivered again. "Come on. It's freezing in here."

"Do you want me to put the lock back?" he asked when they were outside.

"Wait till Mom gets home. She might think it's okay to store stuff in there. I don't see that the house people can object to that, if we're prepared to take the risk. We're really short of space here."

"Isn't there an attic?"

"I don't think so. No one ever said anything about an attic."

"There may be a trapdoor," he said, thoughtfully scanning the landing ceiling, but it was smooth and bare and innocent of trapdoors. He walked slowly along the hall, then stopped outside the door to Hannah's bedroom.

"Ha!" He smiled proudly, and she noticed for the first time that just to the left of the door was a strip of board, about six feet high and a couple of feet wide, screwed to the wall and painted over in the same cream color as the rest of the landing, which was presumably why she hadn't noticed it before.

"Can there be another locked room behind there?" She didn't know whether to be scared or excited.

"Doubt it. It must be covering up something, though. Oh, well." He grinned cheerfully. "Only one way to find out!" And before Hannah could stop him, he had run back to the toolbox and returned with another screwdriver—bigger this time—and set to work.

Remembering his father's previous occupation, she found herself wondering if Mr. Fallon had taught his son to see all barred entrances as a challenge, or if he was just biologically programmed that way.

Even once the screws were out, the board was difficult to dislodge, and in the end Sam had to run the blade of a knife around it before it eventually came unstuck, slightly damaging the paintwork as it did so.

"I hope they don't take that off the deposit," she said dubiously.

"No problem. There's a can of this paint in that room you're not supposed to use. Down on the floor by the door. You can touch it up later."

Hannah wasn't sure if her mother would necessarily feel that redecorating the house was a small price to pay for possible extra storage space, but now Sam had eased the board away from the wall to reveal a proper door behind it. It was painted a dark brown, was very dirty, and had a couple of small holes in the woodwork where the lock and handle had been removed.

"Got a coat hanger?" asked Sam.

Since they'd come as far as this, there seemed little point in stopping now, so Hannah reluctantly fetched the already-bent wire hanger she'd used to fish for the book of fairy tales. "Just remember this wasn't my idea. Okay?" she muttered.

But Sam wasn't listening. He'd inserted the end of the wire hook into the keyhole and was tugging like mad. Suddenly the door shot open, knocking him backward with such force that he cannoned into Hannah and they both landed on the floor in a shower of dust.

"Sorry about that. You okay?" He coughed.

"Just a couple of broken bones and a dislocated shoulder. Nothing serious." She rubbed her arm and stood up, brushing the dust out of her hair. "Seems like you got the door open, at any rate."

They were looking at a flight of uncarpeted stairs that led straight upward to the left, and to what looked like another door at the top.

Sam turned to her, his eyes alight with triumph. "What did I tell you? Every house has an attic!"

He hadn't told her anything of the kind, but she ignored this, as now he was making his way up the steps at as fast a pace as the absence of light would allow, and she seemed to have no choice but to follow. She couldn't help remembering the time, a year and a half ago, when they had discovered another staircase—one that had led down, not up. She had followed him then too. She tried to banish this thought from her mind.

The door at the top of the stairs didn't have a handle either, and it was already slightly ajar. Sam pushed it open, and they walked into a long, narrow room with a sloping ceiling and a grubby casement window with a pane of glass missing. In one corner of the windowsill were half a dozen dead flies. It was hard to see what else was in the room, as everything was covered in a thick, greasy coating of black dust and cobwebs, which concealed its identity as effectively as snow.

When Sam put out a hand to brush away the mess, they discovered a couple of old fire grates, a rusty, tub-shaped object, and a small bathtub lying on its side, displaying clawed feet. The only other contents of the room lay just inside the door or propped against the wall, and seemed to be odds and ends of timber and pieces of broken masonry.

"Doesn't look like anyone's been up here for years," said Sam. "All this junk's ancient."

"There's some space, though. It could be used for storage, I suppose, but I'm not sure Mom will want to." Hannah wrinkled her nose and sneezed. "This dust's getting to me. Let's go down."

"Wait a minute. There's something here. . . ." Sam bent down and reached into the pile of timber. When he straightened up, she saw that he was holding a shallow wooden box.

"What's that?"

"Not sure. Can't see how it opens. Oh. I get it." Applying slight pressure to the lid of the box, Sam slid it fractionally aside. "It's stuck," he muttered. "There are grooves on the inside for the lid to run on, but they're clogged with dirt."

"Can't you get it out?"

"Maybe." Grunting with the effort, he pushed hard on the lid, and it suddenly slid out of its grooves altogether, almost scattering about a dozen colored tablets. "What are they?" he asked, mystified. "Soap?"

Hannah peered closely, running her finger over

one of the tablets. "They're paints! Watercolors. This box is wooden, though, not metal or plastic, so they must be old."

"They're also probably useless. Shall I leave it here?"

"I suppose so." But she continued to look at the little tablets thoughtfully. "That's odd. Whoever used these paints must have had a liking for gloomy subjects."

"Why?"

"Because the bright colors haven't been touched. But the dark blue, the black, and the indigo are almost completely used up."

Sam shrugged. "Since whoever used them probably died years ago, I don't see it matters much." He put the box down on the floor and moved toward the staircase. Hannah was about to follow, giving a final glance around the room, when she spotted something lying in the dust beneath the window.

It was a very small hand. And it was attached to a very small body.

For a moment she stood there, frozen in horror. She couldn't even scream. Then, slowly, she breathed out, as she realized that what she was looking at wasn't the mummified corpse of a baby, but a doll.

THE DOLL

IT LAY FACEDOWN ON the floor as if someone had tossed it there casually. One arm was underneath it, the other outstretched, palm upward. It had long dark hair, stiff with dirt, a dress that had once been white, and the ragged remains of a blue ribbon round its waist. Hannah picked it up and it hung limply, the head and feet seeming too heavy for the soft cloth body.

"Poor old thing," she murmured. "I wonder how long you've been lying here, all forgotten."

"As long as all the rest of this junk, by the look of it," said Sam briskly. "Come on. Are you going to leave it there or bring it with you?"

"I can't just leave her here. Not after we've found her. Maybe I could clean her up somehow."

Back in the kitchen, Hannah laid the doll next

to the sink and, moistening a paper towel under the tap, carefully rubbed at the sooty stains until a face emerged from the grime. A pale porcelain face with a chipped nose, a smiling rosebud of a mouth, and odd brown eyes that stared wildly, as if the owner were not quite sane. She stopped rubbing for a moment, her heart beating fast. Because, for some reason, that odd smile reminded her of something. Then she frowned and shook her head. It was just her imagination. Of course. It had to be.

Even so, it occurred to her that, like the paint box, this doll was old. Very old.

"I think I know who this might have belonged to," she said suddenly.

"What, you mean you can tell just by washing its face?" Sam looked disbelieving, as if she'd claimed to make a genie appear by rubbing a magic lamp.

"I mean I found a book in my bedroom last night. A book of fairy tales. It had the owner's name written inside—Maisie Holt, and the date. Christmas 1876. I think this must have been Maisie's doll."

"Yeah?" Sam was trying to look interested, but he was stifling a yawn and looking pointedly at the refrigerator. "Is it lunchtime yet?"

"Sure. Wait a minute while I fix it." She moved the doll to one side and washed her hands under the kitchen tap, and within ten minutes they were both comfortably settled in front of a video, a plate of sandwiches between them—and Maisie Holt, with her faded, dusty past, temporarily forgotten.

It was only after Sam had gone that Hannah returned to the forlorn figure still lying on the drainboard. She shivered suddenly. It was only a doll, but there was something disturbing about those mad, staring eyes.

Hannah's mother wasn't impressed when she saw the damaged paintwork on the landing, and she was even less impressed by the state of the attic.

"I'm certainly not storing anything in there!" she said, shuddering. "Whatever made you think of unblocking that door?"

"We thought you needed space. It might have been useful. And Sam says there's more of that paint in the other room."

"Which shouldn't have been opened in the first place," replied Mom severely, walking back down the uncovered stairs. "It's a shame we can't use it, though. It would have been the obvious room for us. It's bigger than the other one and gets the light from both windows." She sighed.

"We found something interesting in the attic,"

said Hannah, hoping to distract her. She led the way downstairs and brought the doll from the kitchen.

"Good heavens!" said Mom. "Whatever's wrong with her?" She looked carefully at the pale china face, then laughed suddenly. "Oh, I see. Someone's tried to change the color of the eyes—using a paintbrush, by the look of it. You can just see a bit of the original blue where the new paint hasn't quite covered it. Only there's too much of this brown on her left eye. That's why she looks slightly crazy." She peered closer, lifting the matted hair. "And here's something else. She used to have blond curls—see? They're still underneath. This dark stuff has been stuck on over the top." She rubbed a few strands between her fingers. "What's more, this is real hair. Human hair. Most dolls had hair made of wool in those days. Looks like some little girl had a haircut and then decided to give her doll a makeover with the trimmings!"

"Do you think we could wash her dress?"

"Maybe." Mom sounded doubtful. "Sometimes these things are sewn onto the body." She turned it over. "This isn't, though. Look, it's got a row of buttons at the back. They'll be hard to undo, after all this time." She peered at the tiny buttons and frowned. "Maybe not, after all. Look, these holes are way too big for the buttons. That's unusual. Victorian sewing is usually so neat."

The blue ribbon was a problem, however, and it took a lot of coaxing before the tight little knot yielded at last. Then Mom unfastened the dress and gently pulled it over the doll's head.

"Oh!"

The exclamation came from both Hannah and her mother at once. They stared at the cloth body, naked save for the black boots.

"What's happened to her?" asked Hannah.

"Don't ask me!"

All over the back, stomach, arms, and legs were dark yellowish-brown stains. Each was roughly the size of a small coin, and they were evenly spaced.

"These have been done on purpose, haven't they?" Hannah said in astonishment.

"Looks like it."

"But why?"

Her mother smiled sadly. "I've no idea. Maybe it was some kind of game the child was playing with her friends. Perhaps she thought the marks would wash out and realized too late that they were there to stay. Whatever it was, we're never going to find out now." She put the doll down and looked at her watch. "It's getting late. Do you want to come and help me make dinner?"

"Okay."

Her mother left the room, but Hannah remained looking thoughtfully at the doll. There was something slightly shocking about those pathetic bruised limbs. Because that was just how the marks looked. Like neat, evenly spaced bruises. Gently she ran her finger over one of the marks and noticed that in the center was a tiny hole, the size of a pin. She ran her finger over another and noticed the same thing.

Then she examined the doll carefully. In the center of each stain was a pinhole. Every one. She stared in bewilderment. What kind of game would make a little girl want to stick pins into her doll? And then to disfigure her like this? Would she have gotten into trouble over it? Or did she simply cover it with the dress and hope no one would notice? Suddenly Hannah put the doll down. Her hands were shaking, and she was very cold. The sensation lasted only a few seconds, but it left her feeling sick, as if she had handled something tainted. Something that had gone bad.

Quickly she left the room, closing the door behind her.

A GRAVE DISCOVERY

THE DRIZZLE PERSISTED THROUGH Sunday morning, and Hannah got down to more studying, reading through her notes and memorizing facts, dates, and figures until her brain felt as saturated as the atmosphere outside. But in the afternoon the weather cleared slightly, and she decided to take her sketch pad and go for a walk. Her mother was asleep in a chair, and Hannah closed the front door softly so as not to wake her.

There were few people about. The streets here seemed quieter than those in her own neighborhood, the front gardens free from bikes and swing sets. If children lived here, they must be playing in parks or out for the day. The only sounds were from distant lawn mowers. Otherwise, houses dozed behind half-drawn blinds in the torpid sleepiness of an early-summer Sunday afternoon. She walked for about half a mile before coming to a largish redbrick church, with a gate set in a low wall and a signboard showing times of services. The church itself didn't look very interesting, being Victorian like the houses it served, but it was surrounded by a neatly kept graveyard with flowering shrubs, a path, and one or two wooden seats.

Having found in the past that churchyards sometimes made good drawing subjects, Hannah pushed open the gate and walked slowly along the path, glancing at the gravestones. Those nearest the church were the most recent, with sharp-edged lettering and fresh flowers in small wired pots. Farther back, the stones were older and the inscriptions harder to read. Soon Hannah found she had left the path and was wandering from grave to grave, reading names and dates and wondering how Maria Elizabeth Coombes—who had survived her husband, Albert Samuel Coombes, by more than thirty years—had coped with the rest of her life without him. Had she lovingly cherished his memory, bringing flowers to his grave each Sunday, waiting at last to join him? Or had she dried her eyes, shrugged her shoulders, and gone on with bringing up their seven children, all of whom were now buried nearby?

Then there was Grace Amelia Mason, who didn't appear to have had a husband at all and had died in 1903 at the age of forty-eight. Had she chosen not to marry, or had there been a fiancé who had died in a tragic accident, and Grace Amelia had sworn never to love another?

And there were the tiny graves belonging to the very young children and the babies, some of whom had survived only a few days. Hannah's thoughts went to her brother, Tom, born two years before her, who had lived for only six hours. Her mother had at last come to terms with his death, but she would never entirely get over it. Parents didn't, it seemed. Looking at these small, overgrown mounds, she felt the terrible weight of sadness that was now buried and forgotten.

At last she straightened up and looked at her watch, feeling slightly ridiculous for getting emotional over all these unknown, long-dead people. She wandered back in the direction of the path, and as she did so, her eye caught a name she recognized.

MAISIE HOLT

For a moment, Hannah felt a sense of shock, as though reading about the death of an acquaintance. Then she recovered. Of course. Maisie had lived here, and it was reasonable to suppose she had died here as well. Hannah moved closer and peered at the writing. There wasn't much—just Maisie's name and, underneath, the dates.

BORN MARCH 4, 1866
DIED JUNE 23, 1877

She stared. Could that be right? But the lettering, though worn, was clear enough. Maisie Holt had died at the age of eleven.

Hannah stayed there for perhaps ten minutes, looking at the grave, as if looking closely would somehow reveal more. But there was no more.

At last she moved away. Somehow she didn't feel like sketching anymore.

When she got back, her mother was awake, but she still looked tired, and Hannah decided not to tell her about what she had found in the churchyard. A child's grave was too close to home. But because it occupied her thoughts, she found it hard to talk about anything else, and after an evening meal during which neither of them said much, she cleared the table, stacked the dishwasher, and decided to go to bed, hoping to get to sleep before it got quite dark.

After an hour or so of tossing and turning, she switched on the bedside lamp. If she couldn't sleep, she might as well read. The trouble was, her novel was in her schoolbag, which she had left downstairs, and to fetch it would mean turning on the landing light, which would probably wake Mom. A box of her own books was in the corner, still taped and waiting to be unpacked, but she didn't want to start anything new. Glancing around the room, she noticed the book of fairy tales on the mantelpiece where she had left it two nights ago. The stories were bound to be ones she'd read years ago and would be far too young for her now, but at least they might send her to sleep. She got up, fetched the faded volume, and sat back against her pillow.

A quick glance down the table of contents told her that she'd been right about the stories being familiar. All the old favorites were there—"Sleeping Beauty," "Snow White," "Little Red Riding Hood," "Hansel and Gretel"—as well as one or two she didn't know so well. In spite of herself, she was soon absorbed in the tales of wicked stepmothers, evil queens, cunning witches, and predatory wolves.

It might have been that she was already too wound up by the events of the weekend to let herself relax, but soon Hannah found that, far from sending her to sleep, the stories were making her more jittery. For the first time it struck her how threatening they all were. These were nothing like the stuff written for modern kids, whose characters' problems tended to center around who would be picked for the football team or how to deal with an annoying little sister. They were, literally, stories of life and death. Particularly death. The colored illustrations were beautiful, and of a very high quality, but they were almost too real—too explicit. It was as if the artist and storyteller had colluded in creating a nightmarish world where no one could ever feel quite safe.

Eventually Hannah closed the book and lay down. But it wasn't until the early-summer dawn had begun to filter through the curtains that she at last fell asleep.

NIGHTMARE

Monday MORNING, SCHOOL DRAGGED interminably, and Hannah found it difficult to concentrate. When the bell rang for morning break, she breathed a sigh of relief and went outside to get some fresh air. Sam was waiting for her.

"Are you wearing makeup?" he asked suspiciously.

"No. Why?"

"Your eyes look all black."

"I didn't sleep well. Listen. You know I said that doll we found belonged to a girl called Maisie Holt?"

He nodded, but without much interest.

"She died. I found her grave in the churchyard."

"Well, obviously she died, right? If she hadn't, she'd have been around a hundred and fifty by now, wouldn't she?"

"She died when she was eleven."

He raised his eyebrows, then shrugged. "Kids were always dying young in those days. They died of things like measles and appendicitis."

"And there's something else. The doll's got these brown marks all over it, and each one's got a tiny hole in the center, like there'd been a pin in there."

"Acupuncture?"

"Don't be stupid! The Victorians didn't do acupuncture!"

"Okay, okay, only kidding. Wait a minute! What's happening over there?" He ran off suddenly, heading for the opposite side of the playground, where some kind of disturbance seemed to be going on. Hannah didn't follow but watched him approach a little knot of what looked like younger children, all making a lot of noise and waving their arms. A minute or so later he was back, looking baffled.

"What's up?"

"I'm not sure." He frowned. "One of the year-seven kids had fallen over. That little guy with the fair hair and the glasses. Henry something or other."

"Henry Knight?"

"That's the one."

"Is he okay?"

"Seems to be."

50

"Then what's the problem?"

"The problem is that the other kids think he didn't just fall. He was pushed."

"Who by?"

"Guess."

"Not that new boy? Bruce Myers?"

"Afraid so."

"But Henry just says he fell over?"

"Yes . . . but the others in his class think he might have been saying that because he was scared of what Bruce might do to him later if he told the truth."

"Oh." Hannah frowned. "So what did you do?"

"Nothing. If Henry's not going to make any accusations, there's no point."

She sighed and started to walk back into the school. It was bad enough having exams in this hot term, without all these other problems as well.

As soon as she got home that afternoon, Hannah collapsed in a chair and closed her eyes. The effect of two very short nights made it feel like the end of the week, but it was only Monday.

"Are you all right?" asked Mom anxiously. "You're not sick, are you?"

"I'm all right." Hannah opened her eyes. "Just tired. Are you okay, Mom? You don't look so good yourself."

"I wish your father were here, that's all."

Hannah nodded. She missed Dad too. When he'd been there, the house had seemed too small. Now it seemed too large for just herself and her mother. She'd emailed him a couple of times but hadn't mentioned Maisie or the dreams. There was no point in worrying him, and in any case, what could he do from four thousand miles away?

After dinner she couldn't face doing any work and switched on the TV, flicking aimlessly through the channels. But her mind was too occupied to concentrate on anything, and after fifteen minutes she gave up and went to bed.

It had begun to rain again. She closed the window, opened the curtains, got into bed, and lay on her back listening to the sound of the wind in the trees and the raindrops pattering against the pane. The noise soothed her, and she closed her eyes.

It wasn't raining in the wood. The sun was shining, the birds singing, the fire gently crackling—and surrounding her on all sides were the leaves. Ash leaves. She could see clearly how the delicate, pointed spindles grew on either side of the long stems, each with a single, crowning leaflet curving gently toward its neighbor. The sky between them was light but overcast, which was strange, because surely only bright sunlight could make the green so intense, so vivid. Turning her head, she saw again that smiling face. She lay quite still, watching the face, but it didn't move. It simply stared back through odd, sightless eyes.

But it wasn't the face that, just then, gave her a sudden prickle of unease. It was something else. A faint stirring among the trees. A dark shadow moved there. Was it the wind, shifting the branches? But the leaves were motionless. There was no wind. An animal, then? She strained her eyes to make it out, and as she did so, the shadow became a shape. A shape that broke free from the trees and slowly moved toward her until she saw that it was no animal but a human figure. A woman wearing a long dress and carrying a cup.

She wanted to run away, to escape from that cup, because it was meant for her, she knew that, and she also knew that *she must not drink from it!*

But she couldn't move—her limbs were leaden, claylike. She could only lie there and wait, helplessly, while the woman drew closer and closer until at last the cup was thrust toward her. She grasped it with both hands and hurled it violently into the depths of the wood.

The sunlight faded, the fire ceased its crackling, the leaves vanished, and she was awake, back in her room at Cowleigh Lodge. She sat up against the pillows, sweating and trembling. The strange chemical smell was there again, and the room felt unbearably stuffy, drying her mouth and giving it an unpleasant, bitter taste. She turned toward the little polished bedside cabinet. On the white cloth stood a china basin painted with pink rosebuds, and inside it was a pitcher full of water. Next to them was a glass. She reached eagerly for the pitcher, and as she did so there was a crash. She groped for the white cloth, expecting it to be drenched. But the surface her hand met was quite dry.

And it wasn't polished. In fact, it wasn't a cabinet at all. It was her own painted bedside table. There was no cloth. No pitcher. No basin. Only her alarm clock, and the reading lamp, overturned. With a trembling hand, she set it the right way up and switched it on.

She sat there until at last the shaking subsided enough for her to get out of bed and open the window, leaning out onto the sill and letting the rain wet her face and the sleeves of her pajama top.

At last she got back into bed. It had been the finding of that doll that had transformed this dream into a nightmare, she tried to tell herself. Somehow, her sleeping brain had connected it with those earlier dreams, turning its face into the one she had seen before. And the woman with the cup was fairy-tale stuff, obviously, probably brought on by reading that old book.

But the pitcher, the cloth, the basin? She had really seen those, she was certain. Her eyes had been wide open. Perhaps she had still been in some kind of half-sleeping, half-waking trance?

Yet underneath was another fear. Cold and lurking. For somehow she had *expected* that those things would be beside her. Even before she turned her head, she had known they would be there.

GREEN LEAVES

"I NEED TO TALK to you," she muttered urgently to Sam when he arrived in class that morning.

"Go on then."

"Not now, later. Can we have lunch together?"

"Sure." He looked puzzled. "Is something wrong?"

"Only in my head." Her voice was grim, and he looked at her curiously but said no more.

When lunchtime came, they took their trays to the back of the cafeteria, where there was a table that most people avoided because it had wobbly legs and was in a draft from a side door, but where they had the advantage of being able to talk undisturbed.

"Well?" asked Sam after sitting down and winding spaghetti around his fork. "What's the problem?"

Hannah looked down at her own plate and pushed

it away. "It's Maisie Holt," she said quietly. "I think I'm having her dreams."

Sam's fork drooped, allowing the spaghetti to slowly unwind and slither back to his plate. "What are you talking about?"

She sighed and took a deep breath. This wasn't going to be easy. "The dreams started about a week after we moved in. Then suddenly they stopped. That's why I didn't bother telling you before. Only on Friday night I had another one. And another last night."

She glanced up, but Sam wasn't looking at her. He was winding another forkful. So she went on.

"I'm lying on my back in some kind of wood or forest, because there are green leaves everywhere. Ash leaves, with the sun shining on them. And somewhere there's a fire lit. I can't see it, but I can hear it. And there's somebody with me. It has this weird smile."

"It?"

"What?"

"It. You said 'it.' Why not 'they'?"

"Because . . . because it looked exactly like that doll! Okay, okay, I know what you're going to say," she went on defensively. "That I dreamed about it because we'd found the doll a couple of days before and it was probably still on my mind, but that doesn't explain how I came to dream about that face *before* we found it. I tried to tell myself it was just imagination, but the fact is I saw it, Sam. It was with me in the wood!"

Sam, having successfully negotiated the laden fork to his mouth, chewed thoughtfully for a few moments. Then he swallowed.

"Is that it?"

"No. Not quite. Last night, there was another person. They were walking toward me, holding a cup. But when I took the cup, I didn't drink from it. I just threw it away."

"Was it a nightmare?" he asked after she seemed to have finished.

Hannah thought about it. "No," she said, frowning. "At least, not at the time. It was only after I'd woken up that I was scared, like it had *been* a nightmare. Does that make sense?"

"Mmm. Kind of. What makes you think they're not your own dreams?"

"Because last night, after I'd woken up, I saw things in the room . . . old-fashioned things, which weren't there. Except they were there and they weren't old, they were quite new, and . . . they were familiar, as if . . ." She paused as her voice shook. "As if I was seeing them through somebody else's eyes!"

"How do you know you were awake when you saw them, and not still dreaming?"

"Because I'd already woken up. My eyes were open. I was still shaking!"

"Or maybe you only dreamed you'd woken up. Isn't that a bit more likely?"

She sighed and shook her head. "I don't know. Those things seemed so real. I could have touched them." Then she remembered that when she'd tried to pick up the glass, her hand had simply knocked over the lamp. Perhaps Sam was right after all.

"There's something else." She reached into a plastic bag on her lap and produced the book of fairy tales.

Sam put down his fork and took the book from her. He spent some minutes turning the pages. When he came to the illustrations, he looked searchingly at them. Then he gave the book back and picked up his fork.

"I suppose you're saying that this kid Maisie read these stories, or maybe had them read to her, at bedtime, with her doll beside her, and they gave her the same nightmares you're having now?"

"It's possible, isn't it?"

"And she would have looked at, or been shown, the pictures?"

"Of course."

"Right, then. These leaves you see. The ash leaves. Could you draw them? Were they that clear?"

"I . . . I think so. Yes."

Sam picked up a paper napkin from her tray, found a stub of pencil in his pocket, and put both on the table in front of her. "Here, try it."

She closed her eyes for a few moments. Then she opened them and pulled the napkin toward her. The drawing took only a few seconds. She turned it around, and he stared at it hard before glancing through the book's illustrations, one by one.

"Nope," he said at last, shaking his head. "I don't see anything here to connect your leaves with this book."

"But look at the stories! You must have read them before. What do almost all of them have in common? A wood! And in that wood is something scary. Something that means harm to the child!"

"What are you afraid of, exactly? More dreams?"

Hannah looked bleakly at her untouched plate. "Yes."

"You think the next thing that's going to appear is the big bad wolf? The wicked fairy?"

If it was an attempt to make her lighten up, it failed.

"It's not just the dreams."

"What else?"

"The doll. It . . . I don't know, it feels *wrong* somehow."

He grinned. "So would you feel if you'd had a load of pins stuck in you."

"But Maisie *died*, Sam," persisted Hannah. "She died a few months after getting that book."

Sam swallowed his last mouthful and laid the fork carefully on the plate. He looked up. "Okay, I give in. What you need to do now is try to find out *how* she died. You never know—there could be someone who knows something about the history of that house. But right now, I think you should eat some lunch."

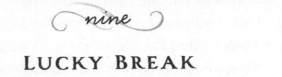

LUCKY BREAK

IT WAS ALL VERY well for Sam to airily issue advice, thought Hannah, but how exactly was she going to find out anything about the death of a child after so much time had gone by? Unless that death had been suspicious, there would be no newspaper reports to look back on, and in any case, with exams approaching she couldn't afford to go investigating anything that didn't have to do with schoolwork.

Besides, over the next week the weather improved. The days were sunnier, the nights lost their close heaviness, and she slept well. For the time being, at least, there was no recurrence of the dreams.

And then, one evening toward the end of the following week, something rather unexpected happened.

She had gone to the local grocery store to buy

lettuce to go with dinner and had just put it down on the counter when the woman serving looked at her curiously.

"Are you the one who's moved into Cowleigh Lodge?"

"That's right."

"Everything okay, is it?" The woman rang up the lettuce on the register.

"Fine, thanks."

"Staying long?"

"Just for a few months, probably."

The woman raised her eyebrows. "That'll be a first, then."

"A first? How d'you mean?" Hannah looked puzzled.

"First time I've known anyone to stay beyond the end of June. Long as I've been here, that place has lain empty through July and August. Then new folk move in around September."

"D'you know why?"

"Roof's in a bad state, could be one reason." The woman stuffed the lettuce into a paper bag and held out her hand. "People always seem to move out after a spell of wet weather. They should get it fixed. Sixty pence, please."

Hannah handed over the money. Then an idea

occurred to her. She glanced behind her to check there wasn't a queue, but there was only an old man propped against the counter reading a newspaper. She turned back. "I don't suppose you know anything . . . anything about the history of that house, do you?"

"History?" The woman looked baffled. "It's Victorian, if that's what you mean. Same as all the other houses in that road."

"Yes. Yes, of course. Well, thanks anyway." Hannah picked up the lettuce and was about to leave when the old man leaning against the counter looked up from his newspaper.

"You could try asking Eileen Grocott," he said.

"What, old Mrs. Grocott down in Laurel Drive?" The woman leaned over the counter to straighten some newspapers. "What'll she know about it, Jim?"

"Her grandmother used to work up at Cowleigh Lodge. Way back."

"How far back?" Hannah felt a little stab of excitement.

"Well . . ." The old man sucked his teeth thoughtfully. "Eileen must be close on a hundred now, I'd think, but her gran was just a young girl when she was in service up there. . . ." He shook his head. "You work it out."

Hannah was bad at math, but even she could

calculate that if the old lady had been born in, say, 1915, her grandmother might have been born around fifty years earlier, which could well have made her a young girl at roughly the time Maisie had died. "D'you think I could go and see her?" she asked. "Would she talk to me?"

The old man shrugged. "You could try. Number three, Laurel Drive. Down by the gas station. Lives with her daughter. Mrs. Wilson's her name, but she's a widow now, so it's just the two of them there."

Hannah thanked him and left the shop. Walking home, she could hardly believe her luck. Sam had said she should find out about the history of the house, and the opportunity had fallen into her lap! Now that the dreams seemed to be a thing of the past, the thought of finding out more about Maisie Holt didn't feel frightening anymore, just intriguing. Today was Thursday. If she went to the house on Saturday morning, with luck someone would be in.

It was much later that evening when it struck her that something the shop woman had said didn't seem to quite add up. If the problem with Cowleigh Lodge was just a leaking roof, why would that be worse in June than at any other time of year? Then she dismissed it. It was odd, certainly, but probably not important.

MRS. GROCOTT

At three o'clock on Friday afternoon, the school entrance hall was full of people planning things to do together on the weekend. Most people, anyway. Hannah noticed that Bruce Myers was standing by himself near the front door. She was gathering the courage to go and speak to him when Sam came careering down the corridor, expertly dribbling a piece of balled-up paper like a soccer ball. It landed neatly at Hannah's feet and he grinned at her. "What are you doing this weekend?"

"Well, tomorrow morning I'm going to visit someone who might be able to fill me in on what happened to Maisie Holt."

"Cool! Can I come?"

Hannah bit her lip. "It might be better if you didn't."

Introducing Sam unexpectedly to what must by now be a very frail old lady didn't seem like a good idea. The shock might kill her. "Tell you what, though," she said, seeing the disappointed expression on his face. "Why don't you come over to my house after lunch? Then I can tell you what I've found out."

"Okay." He seemed satisfied with the compromise, and they parted at the school gates.

By the time she woke up on Saturday morning, Hannah felt a lot less confident about the approaching visit. For all she knew, Mrs. Grocott could be bedridden or suffering from dementia by now, and even if she wasn't, how would her daughter react to a complete stranger knocking on her door and demanding information?

But now that the opportunity was there, she couldn't simply ignore it, so after breakfast she set off through the village until she came to the gas station on the main road. Laurel Drive was a small street just beyond it, lined with about a dozen modern bungalows. When Hannah got to number three, she stood on the doorstep for a moment or so, nervously rehearsing what she was going to say. Then she rang the bell.

A tall, bony woman with tightly waved gray hair and glasses with dark red frames opened the door. She wore brown slacks, a fawn cardigan, and a pair of bedroom slippers.

"Mrs. Wilson?"

"Yes?"

"I'm Hannah Price. My family has rented Cowleigh Lodge for a few months, and I was told that there was a Mrs. Grocott living here who might be able to tell me something about the history of the house."

"That's Mother," said the woman, her face brightening now that she realized Hannah wasn't trying to sell her anything. "Her gran used to be a nursery maid up at Cowleigh Lodge."

"Is she in?"

"Mother, you mean? Oh, she's in, all right. Doesn't go out much now. Was it something in particular you wanted to know about the house?"

"Not really," said Hannah, trying to sound casual. "I just thought it would be fun to find out something about the people who'd lived there."

"Oh, well, you may be lucky. She can't always recall what she's had for breakfast, but she can often tell you all sorts of things that happened eighty years back! Come in, anyhow. My name's Pat, by the way."

Hannah followed her into a small, cluttered living room that seemed to be all curtains and cushions and rugs. A sofa and two armchairs were arranged in front

68

of an electric heater, and in one of the armchairs sat a very old lady, covered in so many shawls and blankets that she looked like part of the upholstery. Her eyes were closed and her breathing came in short rasps.

"Mother!" Pat Wilson put a hand on her shoulder and shook it gently.

The old woman's eyes opened, but they looked cloudy and unfocused. It was hard to tell how much she could see.

"There's a young lady to see you. She wants to know about Cowleigh Lodge."

Mrs. Grocott's jaw worked up and down rhythmically, as if she were chewing something. "Have I had my dinner?" she asked.

"It's not dinnertime yet; you've only just had your breakfast," replied her daughter patiently. She turned to Hannah. "We get this all the time. Doesn't necessarily mean you won't get anything else, if you're prepared to wait. Sometimes it's just a question of saying the right word—something that jogs her memory." She leaned forward and raised her voice slightly.

"Cowleigh Lodge, Mother! Where your gran was nursery maid. She talked to you about what went on up there, didn't she?"

"Yes," said the old lady unexpectedly. Then she looked away. Apparently that was all they were going to get. Meanwhile, Mrs. Wilson drew up a chair for Hannah so that she could sit closer. Hannah thanked her, sat down, and leaned forward. "Mrs. Grocott, did she say anything about the family who lived there? Their name was Holt."

Mrs. Grocott turned her head and seemed to notice Hannah for the first time. "Do I know you?"

Hannah shook her head. "I've just moved here. I'm living at Cowleigh Lodge." She began to feel they were going around in circles. Somehow she needed to find the right words. On an impulse, she took the old lady's hand. "A little girl lived there. Her name was Maisie. Maisie Holt."

Whether it was the pressure of her hand or the name, or a combination of both, she couldn't tell, but suddenly Mrs. Grocott's eyes opened wider, and a shrewd intelligence could be seen lurking behind the cloudy film.

"She died, poor child."

"Do you know how she died?" Hannah felt a sudden twinge of excitement.

"She was ill," replied the old lady, as if this were explanation enough.

"What was wrong with her?"

"My mouth's dry," she complained, turning toward her daughter.

"I'll get you a cup of tea. I expect you'd like one too, wouldn't you, dear?"

"Thank you." Hannah didn't want tea, but it seemed a good way of keeping the conversation going long enough to get as much information as she could.

"What was wrong with Maisie?" she repeated.

Mrs. Grocott was quiet for a few seconds, and then a word shot out of her mouth like a pellet.

"Stomach."

"Stomach?"

"Terrible cramps she had. And vomiting. Poor little mite."

Hannah raised her eyebrows. So maybe Sam had been right about appendicitis after all. That would fit.

Then a thought occurred to her. "Your grandmother was a nursery maid. Does that mean she nursed Maisie when she was ill?"

Mrs. Grocott's mouth pursed in a frown. "Nursery maid was more like maid than nurse. Besides, she wasn't much more than a child herself. Changing linen was her job. That, and fetching fresh water for washing the little girl. Up and down those stairs day and night, she was. There was no bathroom then, see? Water had to be brought in a pitcher and poured into a basin. Besides, there was that other one."

"Which other one?"

But now her wrinkled eyelids were drooping. That last speech seemed to have worn the old lady out.

Mrs. Wilson appeared with a tray and three teacups. She glanced at her mother, then put the tray down.

"We'll just leave her for five minutes," she said. "Then I'll wake her. She dozes all the time. You may still be lucky."

But the sound of the teacups had already woken Mrs. Grocott. She opened her eyes, sat up in the chair, and took the cup from her daughter. It rattled alarmingly in the saucer as her hands shook, but she managed to raise it to her lips and drank noisily. When she put the cup down, her eyes were focused once more.

Hannah waited a few seconds, then asked the question again. "You said there was someone else. Someone else who nursed Maisie when she was ill?"

"Well, of course! There was Miss Holt, wasn't there?" Mrs. Grocott's voice sounded stronger now, even slightly indignant, as though Hannah hadn't been paying attention. The tea seemed to have revived her and sharpened her brain.

"Do you mean Mrs. Holt?" asked Hannah. "Maisie's mother?"

"*Miss* Holt," repeated the old lady severely. "Captain Holt's sister. She lived with them as a kind of governess to Maisie, on account of never having got married herself. And not surprising, Gran used to say. She was a difficult woman."

"How was she difficult?" asked Hannah, sensing something interesting here.

"Always finding fault. Interfering with the way the house was run. Not that it was her place to say." Mrs. Grocott sniffed disapprovingly. "When Maisie got ill, she insisted on taking over the nursing of her. Even prepared her meals for her. Cook was so put out about it, she near gave notice, I'm told! *And* Miss Holt wanted to move the child in with her—I believe she got her way over that right at the end."

"You mean Maisie didn't die in the little room at the back of the house?"

"No. She died in Miss Holt's room. That was when all the talk started."

At first Hannah was so relieved to find that Maisie hadn't died in the room she herself slept in that she didn't take in the second part of this. Then it dawned on her that Mrs. Grocott had just said something significant.

"What talk?"

"Talk among the other servants. They didn't like Miss Holt."

"But Miss Holt wasn't a servant. She was Maisie's aunt."

"She acted as governess. Taught the child her lessons and that. She was a clever woman, I believe, but those who had no husbands and no money were second-class citizens in those days—not like now. Whatever she thought of herself, the servants knew she was one of them. Besides, she was Captain Holt's sister, not his wife's, and the two of them never got along."

Hannah felt a moment's pity for Miss Holt, who seemed to have been liked by no one.

"What was all the talk about? After Maisie died?"

But the eyes had begun to cloud over again. The jaw hung loose, and Hannah watched helplessly as the old lady seemed to slip away into a light doze.

She heard the door click and looked up to see Mrs. Wilson coming in. Hannah hadn't even noticed her leaving the room, but now she reappeared, holding something.

"I knew I'd find it if I looked hard enough." After shifting the teacups to one side and wiping a space with a tissue, she laid a brownish photograph on the table. It was mounted on stiff card and showed a group of six people posed on some steps at the back of what was still recognizable as Cowleigh Lodge. All were female—two were seated, wearing long skirts and light-colored blouses with high necks and full sleeves, and four were standing. Two of these wore black dresses with white aprons; a third had a lighter-colored dress with an apron but no cap.

But it was the sixth person who immediately caught Hannah's attention. This was a slender little girl of about nine or ten, in a knee-length white dress with a deep-frilled hem and broad sash. A cloud of dark hair fell loose to her shoulders, drawn back from a high forehead above widely spaced, intelligent eyes. Her nose was small and straight and her mouth full, the gently curving lips slightly parted—and cradled in her arms was a doll. A doll with fair curly hair.

"That's Maisie, isn't it?" Hannah's voice was excited. "And this must be the doll we found in the attic! It's got dark hair now, but this blond stuff's still underneath."

Mrs. Wilson raised her eyebrows. "You don't say! Still there after all that time? Well, well . . . who'd have thought it? Anyhow, you're right, this is Maisie, of course. Pretty little thing, wasn't she? And a little angel, by all accounts. Mind you, people always say that about a child that's died, don't they?"

"Angel," muttered a voice from the armchair.

"You with us again, Mother?" Pat Wilson smiled encouragingly. "I was just saying that Maisie was a good little girl, wasn't she?"

There was no reply. Her daughter turned back to the photograph. "And this one here"—she pointed to one of the standing figures wearing a cap—"is my great-grandmother."

Her voice had a note of pride, and Hannah dutifully dragged her gaze away from Maisie to the young girl, about fourteen or so, who stood with her feet together and her hands folded demurely in front of her. She regarded the camera with a wary expression, as though at any minute she expected it to explode.

"Then this would have been the housemaid," continued Mrs. Wilson, pointing to the other capped girl, "and this one here was the cook. She's not wearing a cap, to show she's senior to the maids."

Hannah frowned. "It seems like a lot of servants for quite a small house. It's hardly big enough for me and my parents!"

"Don't forget you've got a bathroom now. That would have been a bedroom in those days. And there's an attic, isn't there? That's where my great-grandmother slept, with the housemaid here. People didn't have so many possessions in those days, and they expected to sleep two to a room, often."

Hannah thought of the grimy, cobweb-filled loft and tried to imagine it as a neat, plainly furnished bedroom shared by two young girls not much older than herself, perhaps. Would they have whispered and giggled as they lay in bed, gossiping about what went on in the rest of the house?

She stared at the photograph, and for the first time properly noticed the two seated figures. "Is one of these Maisie's mother?"

"That's her." Mrs. Wilson pointed to a pretty, dark-haired woman who, unlike the others, wasn't looking at the camera at all. She seemed abstracted, as if the photographer had caught her when she wasn't ready and was thinking about something else.

"Angela," said Mrs. Grocott unexpectedly.

"What's that, Mother? Mrs. Holt's name wasn't Angela." She shook her head. "Getting confused now. Not surprising."

"She looks just like Maisie," said Hannah. "Mrs. Holt, I mean."

Pat Wilson frowned and seemed about to say something, but then appeared to change her mind. She pointed to the second figure. "And this one's Miss Holt."

"Maisie's aunt?"

"That's right. No oil painting, was she? No wonder she never found a husband!"

Miss Holt had a narrow, pinched face, thick black eyebrows, a long, pointed nose, and a jutting chin. In between, her mouth had an expression of angry disapproval. It was hard to see how this woman could possibly have been the aunt of that pretty child, but quite easy to see why she might have been unpopular.

"Where's Maisie's father?" asked Hannah. "Do you know why he wasn't in the photo?"

"Captain Holt was a soldier. He was away a lot, fighting some war or other, and got himself killed soon after Maisie died. I rather doubt he even knew what had happened to her, which was just as well, considering." Again Mrs. Wilson frowned, and Hannah sensed it was the right time to ask the question she'd tried to put to Mrs. Grocott.

"Your mother said that after Maisie died, there was talk among the servants. Do you know what she meant?"

Mrs. Wilson glanced at the old lady in the chair, whose eyes were closed once more. "You've got to remember," she began slowly, "that feelings run high when a child dies. And everyone loved Maisie, I believe. The trouble was, so far as I can tell, that this Miss Holt took all the nursing on herself, and when the little girl died, everyone looked for someone to blame."

"They thought she'd let her die unnecessarily?"

"Worse than that."

Hannah stared at her. "You can't mean . . . ?"

Mrs. Wilson nodded. "It seems crazy, doesn't it? What did she have to gain from the child's death? All the same, the servants got it into their heads that she'd deliberately done away with that little girl."

"But were they right?"

Mrs. Wilson simply spread her hands helplessly. "How can anyone be certain, after all this time? Nothing was ever proved, that's all I know."

"So if she did"—Hannah swallowed—"deliberately kill Maisie, she got away with it?"

"I wouldn't say that, exactly. Miss Holt might not have been found guilty officially, but the result was much the same as if she had been. Word got around, you see, and after Maisie died, no one would employ her aunt. I believe eventually she ended up in the workhouse, and she died there shortly after."

Hannah shivered. She had heard of conditions in Victorian workhouses. Then a thought struck her. "Did Maisie's mother think she was guilty too? Is that why she couldn't stay on at Cowleigh Lodge?"

Mrs. Wilson's face flushed. "No one stayed on after Maisie died. Mrs. Holt moved away and the house was sold."

Hannah looked curiously at her, wondering why she seemed suddenly ill at ease. Was it the thought of

Maisie's mother, living out the rest of her life with her only child dead and no husband to support her? Whatever the truth, it was a depressing story. But there was still something she needed to know.

"Did Maisie . . . did she ever say she had dreams? Nightmares?"

"Nightmares? Not that I know of. What kind of nightmares?"

"About being in a wood. Surrounded by leaves."

"I daresay she might have been delirious toward the end. Is that what you mean?"

"No. I don't think so. It doesn't matter." Hannah was about to get up and go, but then she hesitated. "Your mother must have talked to you a lot about all this—for you to know so much?"

Mrs. Wilson nodded slowly. "She has. But, funnily enough, not when I was younger. It's only been in the last ten years or so, as her short-term memory's worsened, that all this past stuff has come out. And I believe it was the same with *her* mother. Grandma never said a word about it till she was quite an old lady, apparently, but it must have been preying on her mind all those years. Oh, well." She smiled sadly. "That'll be the end of it now, anyway. I've no children to tell the story to. My husband and I would dearly have liked some, but we were never blessed."

There was a slightly awkward silence. Then Hannah got up to go. "Would you mind if I borrowed this for a while? I'll take care of it." She pointed to the photograph.

"Of course you can. Hold on to it for as long as you want. And listen"—she looked anxious—"maybe I shouldn't have told you all that about Miss Holt, not when you're living in the house. It won't give *you* nightmares, will it?"

"Well, if it does, it's not your fault. I asked for information, and you gave it to me!"

"Mmm." Mrs. Wilson still looked worried. "Tell you what—I'll give you my cell-phone number. I'm a poor sleeper—comes of living with Mother, I expect. She naps during the day and then wonders why she's awake half the night. If you need to talk, just call me. If I'm not asleep, the phone'll be switched on."

Hannah thanked her. But while she was copying the number, she realized there was one obvious question she still hadn't asked. "Apart from Miss Holt being difficult, and taking over the nursing, what else made the servants suspicious of her?"

Pat Wilson frowned. Then she sighed. "Oh, well, I've told you so much already, I don't suppose one more thing will make much difference. It's just that from time to time, I believe Maisie was covered in bruises. Black and blue, she was. Only nobody could ever explain why."

"And they thought Miss Holt had caused them?" Hannah was shocked. "Did she beat her?"

"I don't think so. That was the point, you see. The bruises just suddenly appeared overnight."

"Angelina!"

They both turned to stare at Mrs. Grocott, who was wide awake now, a look of triumph on her face.

"No, no, Mother," her daughter said patiently. "Miss Holt wasn't called Angelina. You know that."

"Not *her*. Angelina was the name of the little girl's dolly! Knew I'd get there in the end."

Mrs. Wilson chuckled. "So that's what you've been trying to remember, is it? We were wondering what it was all about."

But Hannah refused to be distracted. "You were saying? About the bruises? And the servants?"

"Oh, yes." She laughed nervously. "I expect it was just a lot of nonsense, but for some reason the staff all got it into their heads that Miss Holt was a witch!"

eleven

DRAWING

"A WITCH! ARE YOU serious?" Sam had arrived after lunch, and as soon as her mother went out to the shops, Hannah had taken him straight up to her bedroom, where she had filled him in on what she had discovered about Cowleigh Lodge.

"That's what she said."

"Just because of a few bruises? Why couldn't the kid have gotten them playing in the garden?"

"They appeared *overnight*, Sam. She wouldn't have been playing outside in the middle of the night!"

"Maybe they had some weird connection with her illness?"

"Or maybe the aunt had," she said darkly.

Sam frowned and ran his fingers through his hair, making it stick up in ginger tufts. Then he sighed.

"Okay. I think I get the picture. You're saying that this is what those dreams are all about? That what really scared Maisie wasn't some character in a book, but her own aunt?"

"Well, it makes sense, doesn't it? Maisie suspected her aunt all the time, but never let on. She suppressed it, which is why it could only come out in her dreams!"

"Didn't you say there was a photograph?" Sam said at last.

"It's downstairs. I'll fetch it." When she returned, he took the photo from her and peered at it closely. He pointed to the little girl. "This is Maisie, right?"

"Yes. And that's the aunt, sitting next to her."

Sam opened his eyes wide in mock horror. "Ugh! She's hideous! No wonder the kid was scared of her. She's enough to give anyone nightmares, just looking at her!"

"I suppose she couldn't exactly help the fact she was ugly."

"It could give her a motive, though." He grinned. "Maybe she was jealous. Maisie was quite a looker, wasn't she?"

Hannah nodded thoughtfully, and for the first time she looked at the photograph properly, in a way she hadn't had a chance to do with Mrs. Wilson there.

Apart from Maisie's mother, who hardly looked

as though she was in the picture at all, the grown-ups had a stiff seriousness about them. Photographs at that time were clearly no laughing matter, and the servants all gave an impression that they were facing a firing squad. Only Maisie looked alive—vivacious. Hannah looked at the small face, shining with vitality even through the faded sepia: at the lustrous dark brown hair, the pretty white dress with its sash and deep hem. Then she caught her breath.

"What's the matter?" Sam looked up.

Without replying, Hannah ran out of the room and galloped down the stairs. A moment later she was back, holding the doll.

"Look at it!" She thrust it into Sam's hands and he stared in bewilderment.

"What am I meant to be looking at?"

"Her dress!

Sam obediently looked at the doll's dress, then back at Hannah, but his eyes were still baffled. "I don't get it. What's so special about this dress?"

"Now look at the photo. *What is Maisie wearing?*"

Still frowning, he did as he was told. Then, suddenly, light dawned. "It's . . . the same dress."

"Exactly! You can't see from the photo that the sash is blue, like the ribbon, but I wouldn't mind betting it was. And that's not all. The doll used to be blond. This dark hair has been stuck over the top. And the eyes were blue once, only someone's painted them brown!"

The baffled expression was back on Sam's face. "Why would they do that?"

"Don't you see? This doll has been made to look exactly like Maisie!"

"Well, so what? It's the kind of thing girls do, isn't it?"

"And then stick pins in themselves?" Hannah thrust the doll into his hands and at the same time pulled the dress up over the doll's head, revealing the odd yellowish-brown marks, each with its telltale puncture. "Angelina," she muttered.

"What?"

"Mrs. Grocott said that Maisie called it Angelina."

It. She'd said "it" again. Not "her." The hard little word lay between them. There was an uncomfortable silence.

Suddenly Sam dropped the doll. It landed on the floor with a soft thud, and Hannah looked up at him.

"Hey! What's the matter? You okay?" His face had gone deathly white, but sweat beaded his forehead and his hands were shaking.

"Please tell me this isn't what I think it is."

She didn't reply. Instead she stared at the doll

where it had fallen, the dress rucked up to its waist, the painted smile no longer demure but shameless, immodest . . . *bad*.

The beginnings of realization came like a trickle of icy water. Quickly, the trickle became a flood. "Of course! It's an *image*, isn't it? Like a voodoo doll?"

"I don't see what else it can be." Now that Sam was no longer holding the doll, he'd stopped shaking, but his face was still pale. "It's dressed like Maisie, its eyes are like hers, and so is its hair. It's even got her bruises. No wonder it feels evil. It's had a curse put on it!"

"But could this be what killed her?"

"I don't know, but one thing's for sure—it wasn't meant to do her any good!"

For a few moments, neither of them spoke. Then Sam pulled himself together. "You need to get rid of it," he said roughly.

"How?"

"Who cares? Burn it. Throw it in the garbage."

"I . . . I can't do that."

"Why not, for heaven's sake? The kid's *dead*, isn't she? You can't do her any more harm now!"

Hannah swallowed. "I . . . just can't do it, Sam," she muttered.

"Okay, then. We put it back where we found it." Without waiting for a response, he snatched up the limp creature and went out onto the landing. The board covering the entrance to the loft hadn't been screwed back but lay against the brown-painted door. Sam pushed it aside and walked quickly up the stairs. Hannah started to follow, but he turned around. "Go and get that toolbox."

When she returned, he was already back on the landing, waiting for her. In silence, she watched him take the screwdriver and replace the screws, one by one. Then he straightened up again and breathed out, hard. She knew from his face that he was thinking the same as she was. It had felt unpleasantly like sealing up a tomb.

-»»-

Sam didn't stay long that day. The discovery had shaken them both too much for normal conversation, and he left soon after four, telling her that she should call him if she needed to.

In the evening, her mother settled down in a chair with a cup of coffee and the newspaper. Hannah sat with her geography textbook, trying to memorize facts about population density, but she still felt jittery and fidgeted, unable to concentrate.

At last Mom looked up. "Why don't you do some drawing?" she suggested. "I haven't seen you take out your sketchbook for ages."

It was true that the last time she had tried to draw had been the day she'd gone for a walk, the day she'd discovered Maisie's grave in the churchyard. Since then, she simply hadn't felt like sketching, which was unusual. Maybe this was a good time to start again. It might take her mind off things. But what to draw? She needed a subject.

Still wondering, she walked slowly upstairs to her bedroom and pulled the sketch pad out of her school-bag. Then her eye fell on the photograph, lying just where she and Sam had left it, with the face of little Maisie Holt shining out like a bright candle from the somber darkness of the unsmiling figures surrounding her.

Of course! She had found her subject. Just for a second she hesitated, torn between memory of the awful thing in the loft and the immediate, urgent desire to do what she loved best. Then she picked up the photograph, seized her sketch pad, and ran back downstairs.

Mom looked up and smiled as Hannah entered the room.

Settling herself into the chair, she took a long, searching look at the face before her. Again she was struck by its intelligence and vitality. Could she get that onto the page?

But as soon as her pencil began to move, she felt the old, familiar wash of creativity surrounding her, deepening, like warm, sweet water. And then she was afloat.

She worked for perhaps twenty minutes, occasionally correcting a line here, a curve there. But for the most part, the likeness flowed surprisingly easily. Once the face was complete, Hannah added the rest of the figure. Then she sat back and observed what she had done.

It was good. Very good, in fact. She sat back in the chair and closed her eyes. She was used to the sudden release of tension after drawing something that had absorbed her thoroughly. But this was slightly different, though she couldn't quite analyze why.

She opened her eyes and looked again at the face she'd drawn. It looked back at her. Why did she find that gaze disconcerting, suddenly?

SUNDAY

She woke the next morning to a bright, sunny day, with just a faint haze in the distance promising heat to come. As it was Sunday, there was no need to hurry over getting up, so she had a long, lazy bath, during which she had time to observe that several of the tiles were coming unstuck from the bathroom wall. She didn't remember noticing that before but supposed it must be the damp, steamy atmosphere that had loosened them. Or maybe they hadn't been stuck down well enough in the first place. Never mind. That was the real estate agent's problem. After soaking for a further ten minutes, she dried herself, got dressed, and went downstairs feeling relaxed and well rested.

"Morning!" she said cheerfully.

Her mother was standing over the toaster, waiting.

"Morning. Sleep well?"

"Great! You?"

"Mmm. Can you get the butter out?"

As Hannah opened the refrigerator, she dislodged two or three of the magnetic letters stuck to the door and bent down to put them back. "Are you all right, Mom? You sound tired."

"I'm okay." She sighed. "I miss Dad, that's all."

"Me too." Hannah took out the butter and shut the door. Looking at her mother's pale face, she felt a stab of guilt. Lately she'd been so wrapped up in her own concerns that she'd hardly spared a thought for how Mom might be coping. Now was a good time to put that right. "Why don't we have lunch out today?" she suggested. "There's that nice pub near the cathedral—the Black Bear. I'm sure they do food on a Sunday."

"But I bought a chicken. I was going to roast it."

"We can have it tomorrow, can't we? Come on, Mom, it'll do us both good to get out of the house for a while."

At last her mother smiled. "All right. Why not?"

Hannah divided the morning between her geography textbook and a list of chemical equations that needed learning. Yesterday's jitteriness had quite disappeared; her concentration was so much restored that by midday she had covered a satisfying amount of ground and felt she had earned a break.

At twelve thirty she and her mother set off, strolling unhurriedly through the quiet streets, enjoying the warm sunshine. The Black Bear was an old coaching inn on the south side of the cathedral square, popular with tourists because of its dark oak beams, crooked windows, and general air of comfortable dilapidation. Hannah and her mother had a leisurely lunch, then walked for a while by the river, watching children throwing bread to the swans.

It was nearly three o'clock by the time they got back to Cowleigh Lodge. Mom switched on the TV, and Hannah settled down to learn some history notes. After an hour or so, she noticed that a familiar shape was missing from the hearth rug.

"Mom, where's Toby?"

"What?" Her mother glanced around vaguely. "Not sure. Outside, probably."

Hannah frowned. The cat was almost always there when they were watching TV. Come to think of it, she hadn't seen him all day. "Has he eaten his dinner?"

"I don't know. Go and look if you want to." Mom turned back to the screen.

Hannah spent another ten minutes on her history notes, then went out to the kitchen. Toby's bowl was empty, so he must have come in through the cat flap and gone straight out again. She put the kettle on to make a cup of tea and was about to open the refrigerator to get the milk out when something caught her attention on the door. Four of the little magnetic letters stood apart from the others and were roughly grouped together.

HANA

For a few seconds she stood quite still, staring at the door. Then she remembered accidentally knocking a few of the letters onto the floor at breakfast time. She must have put them back like that without realizing. It was odd that it looked a bit like her own name, but just a coincidence. Of course, it had to be.

She took out the milk, put cups and saucers on a tray, and carried it into the other room.

Neither of them felt like eating much that evening, having had a large lunch, so later on, after heating a can of soup, Hannah did another hour's work and then went to bed. When she opened her bedroom door, she noticed that the board covering the fireplace had slightly bowed away from the wall, allowing a faint trace of soot to fall on the carpet. She couldn't be bothered to sweep it up just then, so she left it there. Just before getting into bed, she drew a pencil line through the date on the torn-off calendar page still stuck to the mirror.

June 17. Just over halfway through the month.

ELECTRICAL FAULT

Monday morning dawned bright and clear, and by nine thirty, warm sunshine filtered invitingly through the windows of classrooms where students sat either writing furiously or despondently chewing gel pens, depending on how much preparation they had done.

Hannah was relieved to find she could manage the first exam—geography—with a minimum of pen chewing, and after lunch she joined Sam in the playground for the usual discussion of the morning's test. After chatting for a few minutes, she glanced up and frowned. "There's that boy Henry Knight. What's happened to him this time?"

Henry was surrounded by a group of children from his own class who were clearly agitated about something, but because they surrounded him it was impossible to see what all the fuss was about. She wandered closer. "Everything okay?" she asked a girl with dark pigtails.

"No! Henry's got this massive bruise over his eye. And another one on his wrist. Looks like some-body got hold of him and punched him, but he won't admit it. Just says he walked into a lamppost. As if we'd believe that!" She rolled her eyes dramat-ically.

"Has he been to the nurse?"

"He won't. Says it's not serious enough. But we think it's because he just doesn't want to cause trouble for you know who!" The girl shook her head, making the pigtails quiver in sympathetic indignation.

"Who exactly do you mean?" Hannah knew the answer but was curious to discover what evidence Henry's friends had to make them so certain.

"Bruce Myers, of course! None of this started till he got here."

"Has anyone asked him about it?"

"No way! We're all too scared of him." She turned back to the little group around Henry, and Hannah walked thoughtfully back to Sam, who raised a ques-tioning eyebrow.

"Well?"

She shrugged. "I honestly don't know. Those kids seem convinced that Henry Knight's being beaten up by Bruce Myers, but no one wants to tackle him about it in case they get beaten up too."

Sam looked alarmed. "That's bad! D'you think we should tell someone?"

"I don't see how we can. Like you said before, if Henry won't say what really happened, there's nothing much anyone can do. In any case, the girl I spoke to didn't seem to have any reason for accusing Bruce beyond the fact that he's new to the school and looks scary."

"And, right now, Mr. Unpopular," remarked Sam, jerking his head in the direction of a lone figure standing near the fence. He glanced at his watch. "Come on. Now's our chance to show 'em how much history we don't know!"

When Hannah pushed open the door of Cowleigh Lodge that afternoon, the first thing that struck her, judging by the smell coming from the kitchen, was that they were having roast chicken for dinner. The second thing, judging by the clatter and muttered curses coming from the same place, was that her mother wasn't in a good mood. The reason for this became clear when she saw Mom on her hands and knees, sweeping up the remains of a broken pitcher.

"What happened?"

"The pitcher fell off the shelf," returned Mom

curtly. "Don't ask me how! I wasn't anywhere near it at the time." She finished brushing the pieces into a dustpan and dropped them in the trash.

"It was here, wasn't it?" Hannah examined a shelf near the door, which wobbled slightly. "Oh, I see. The screw's come loose. I'll fix it." She opened the cupboard under the sink, which was where she'd put her father's toolbox, found the screwdriver that Sam had used on the upstairs landing, and tightened the screw. "That should do it."

"Thanks. I'm sorry, sweetheart, I didn't mean to snap just when you get home, but I can't tell you what a frustrating day this has been! Whatever I've tried to do, something's gone wrong. First the vacuum cleaner quit on me. Just stopped working, halfway down the stairs. So I left it and went to fetch a cloth to clean the windows. I started upstairs, and I'd just finished the ones in your bedroom when the vacuum started up again. All on its own!"

"It probably overheated before and you forgot to switch it off," suggested Hannah.

"After half a staircase? Anyway, I finished the vacuuming and set up the board to do some ironing. So I switched on the iron and was just about to go upstairs and fetch the clothes when there was this terrific bang from behind me!"

"The iron? It's broken then?"

"Dead as a doornail. I'll have to buy a new one tomorrow."

"Sounds like the house needs rewiring. It was probably done years ago and no one's checked it recently."

"Maybe. This place has been pretty carefully done up otherwise, though." Mom suddenly put her hand to her mouth. "I forgot! How were the exams?"

"Could have been worse."

"That's good. Come on then, let's eat some of this chicken."

Fortunately, the oven didn't seem to be suffering from any peculiar electrical disorder, and dinner put Mom in a better mood. Afterward, she sat down to listen to a radio program while Hannah loaded the dishwasher. Just before leaving the kitchen, she glanced at the door of the refrigerator, noticing that now the letters were innocently bunched together in one corner where Mom had moved them when she'd been cleaning. Yesterday's random selection had obviously been just that—random.

Hannah went back into the living room and settled in an armchair to look over her science notes for tomorrow. Again, the hearth rug was empty.

"Mom," she said, puzzled. "What's wrong with Toby? I haven't seen him for a couple of days now."

"Don't ask me! I've hardly seen him either. If he didn't come in to eat, I'd suspect someone else was feeding him, but he just comes in for long enough to wolf down his food, then goes straight out again."

Frowning, Hannah considered this. Then she shook her head and went back to her notes. Cats were funny creatures—there was no point trying to figure out what went on in those furry little heads.

At ten o'clock she packed away her books, kissed her mother good night, and went upstairs. As she got undressed, she noticed that the decoration in her room was showing a few signs of wear: The layers of paint and paper curled up very slightly where they met the mantelpiece, and there was another small patch where they had come unstuck near the window. Probably, she thought, the house had been repainted quickly, without too much care about surface preparation. Dad was always saying that was the key to good decorating. Yawning, she crossed off another day on the calendar and got into bed.

She had almost dropped off when the sound of distant laughter seemed to come from somewhere. Upstairs, maybe, but of course it couldn't be upstairs, she thought drowsily. It must be the radio. She should go and ask Mom to turn it down, but she really couldn't be bothered. Not now.

fourteen

DISTURBANCES

Tuesday's weather was hotter. At school, a light breeze blew through the open classroom window, gently ruffling exam papers and making the big hanging map of the world skitter against the wall. Hannah's class was being tested on science both morning and afternoon, and after a day battling with questions on fractional distillation and parallel circuits, she got back to Cowleigh Lodge feeling she'd earned a rest.

But as soon as she'd let herself in, one look at her mother's face told her that all was not well.

"Come and look at this." Mom's voice sounded tight, ominously controlled. She led Hannah upstairs to the bedroom at the front of the house, which she and Dad had taken over. Pushing open the door, she pointed to the top of the wall. All along the side nearest the window, the layers of paint and paper had come loose from the plaster and curled outward stiffly for a distance of about half an inch.

"Now look at the curtains," said Mom, before Hannah could comment on the wallpaper.

The window was open and the curtains were blowing lightly, with one hanging noticeably lower than the other.

"What happened to this?"

"The screw holding the rail's come out of the wall."

"Oh. That's a nuisance. But we can put it back, can't we?"

"And now take a look at the radiator."

Hannah cast an anxious glance at her mother's face before going over to the other side of the room, where it was plain what the problem was this time. The radiator was one of the old-fashioned kind that was designed to be screwed into the wall, but now one of the brackets that were meant to secure it at the top had sheared off, so although it was still joined to the pipe at the bottom, it wobbled freely at one end.

"We . . . we're not using the central heating at the moment, are we?" she said, still hoping to put an optimistic slant on things.

"No, we're not," replied her mother with a brittle smile. "I was, however, still hoping to use this." She walked over to the side of the bed and switched on the reading lamp. Nothing happened.

"Bulb gone?"

"I've changed it."

"Fuse?"

"I've changed that too."

"Maybe we're having a power outage," suggested Hannah, but not very hopefully.

"Then why is the television working? The refrigerator?"

"I don't know, Mom. Perhaps they're on a different circuit or something. Does the main light work?" She moved to the door and pressed the switch. The light came on. "There you are. At least you don't have to go to bed in the dark." She gave an encouraging smile.

But her mother refused to be consoled. "That's not all." She walked over to the window and pointed to the floor. "Look. Over here the carpet's come untacked underneath the window. And have you seen the tiles in the bathroom? The paper in your bedroom? Steph brought Billie around for coffee this morning, and she was horrified!"

"Steph has the kind of house that gets photographed for glossy magazines. She practically faints at the sight of dust," Hannah reminded her patiently. Mom's closest friend, mother of six-year-old Billie, was famously proud of her housekeeping. "Why wasn't Billie in school, anyway?"

"Some bug or other. He seemed lively enough to me." Her mother shrugged. Then she shook her head, frowning. "I just don't get it! How can a house deteriorate so fast?"

Hannah sat down on the bed and looked thoughtfully at her mother. "We've had all the windows open a lot recently, haven't we?"

"Of course. It's been hot outside."

"But before we moved in, they would have been closed. According to the woman in the shop, this house has been hard to rent, so they could have been closed for a long time—don't forget, you said yourself that it felt damp at first. Supposing all this fresh air we're letting in suddenly is drying the house out. Mightn't that make the wallpaper come unstuck, loosen the screws?"

"Maybe."

"What's wrong?"

"Oh, I don't know. There's probably a perfectly good explanation, but for some reason I can't even persuade Toby to come into the house these days. I've had to start leaving his dinner outside the back door."

"Perhaps he still feels unsettled here. He knows it's not his real home."

"Then why was he fine when we first moved in? I don't understand it. Ever since last weekend, he's avoided the house like it had a dog in it!"

Hannah sighed. She felt she'd had enough of trying to solve baffling problems for one day. "Don't worry, Mom, he'll come back when he's ready. But right now, can we have something to eat?"

"Of course. I'm sorry." Mom smiled, and they went downstairs.

Dinner was cold chicken and salad, which they ate at the kitchen table. Afterward, Hannah took her schoolbag up to her bedroom and tipped the books onto the bed. She noticed that more soot had escaped from underneath the boarded-up fireplace, and that the paper above the mantelpiece seemed to have come a little farther away from the wall, but the explanation she had given Mom now felt like the most probable one, and she settled down to concentrate on learning French verbs.

She had been at it for about an hour when a sudden crash from the floor below made her jump. She got up and stuck her head through the doorway. "Mom? Are you okay?"

There was no reply. Quickly she ran downstairs and, having glanced in and seen that her mother wasn't in the living room, discovered her standing in the kitchen, staring down at the smashed remains of a jar of peanut butter.

"Bad luck," said Hannah sympathetically. "Did you drop it?"

"I didn't touch it. It fell out of that cupboard over there." Mom looked shaken. "I suppose I can't have put it back properly after I fixed Billie a snack this morning."

"Look, you go and sit down. I'll take care of this." Hannah shooed her mother out of the kitchen and set to work with the dustpan and brush. After dropping the broken glass in the bin and wiping the floor with a cloth, she straightened up and looked at the cupboard. It was easy to see what had happened this time. Here the shelves weren't screwed in but rested on wooden supports, two of which had shifted slightly, causing the shelf to tip forward. Having pushed the jars and bottles firmly to the back of the shelf, she went to the refrigerator to get a glass of milk. But as she was about to open the door, her attention was held by something on the front of it. For a moment, she froze, her heart thudding. Then she turned round and walked quickly into the living room.

"Mom, when you and Steph were having coffee this morning, where did you sit?"

Her mother looked up, surprised. "In here. Why?"

"Where was Billie?"

"In here too, most of the time."

"Could he have gone into the kitchen on his own?"

"Probably. We were talking. I didn't really notice. He couldn't have reached that peanut butter jar, if that's what you're thinking."

"No. It doesn't matter."

She returned to the kitchen and leaned heavily against the wall. It had been Billie, of course, bored with listening to grown-up talk, looking for something to do. Six-year-old Billie, who was just learning to write.

Who else would have moved the magnetic letters so that they spelled

HELP ME

After a few moments she stepped forward, roughly shuffled the letters into the rest of the collection, and left the kitchen, closing the door firmly behind her. Then she went back upstairs. At nine thirty, she packed her schoolbag and took it down to the hall, leaving it by the front door ready for the morning.

It was when she was in the bathroom brushing her teeth that she noticed the tiles above the bath. They were now so loose that one of them had almost come away from the wall altogether, revealing the yellowish, hardened glue behind. But in one spot there was no glue, and when Hannah peered closer, she could just make out a very faint trace of something else. A pale blue stripe.

She remembered Mrs. Wilson's words. *"Don't forget you've got a bathroom now. That would have been a bedroom in those days."*

There was no reason why the memory of those words should have made her shiver suddenly, any more than the sight of that tiny patch of wallpaper, no bigger than a small coin. Except that for a moment, she felt as though she had been caught guiltily spying through a keyhole. A keyhole into another world.

Quickly she finished brushing her teeth and went to bed.

fifteen

MESSAGE RECEIVED

WEDNESDAY BEGAN ORDINARILY ENOUGH. The weather was still hot and dry and, according to the forecast, set to remain so until the weekend. Hannah had slept well. Walking to school, she felt well prepared for the day's exam.

The French exam was straightforward, and by the time she put down her pen at twelve thirty, she knew she'd done okay and could enjoy lunch with a clear conscience. There was no exam set for the afternoon—instead the class was expected to do some private study in the library, and at one thirty she and Sam sat down side by side to get ready for the following day. Hannah had made some notes in her English notebook the night before and now opened it.

For one puzzling moment she thought she'd made a

mistake and picked up someone else's book. But there was her name on the front, and a brief glance over the notes showed her own work of the night before. There was no mistake.

Only, some way below her own writing, in a looped, spidery script, three words were penciled.

Let me go

Trying to control a rising sense of panic, she sought an explanation. Somebody at school had taken the notebook and played a trick on her. Or maybe someone had picked up her notebook by accident and written in it before realizing their mistake. But even as she tried to convince herself, she knew it wasn't possible. The book had been in her schoolbag ever since she'd put it there last night. And her schoolbag hadn't left her side all morning.

Hannah stared at the words as they swam before her eyes. Her heart was pounding. Roughly she pushed the notebook away from her, put her elbows on the table, and covered her face with her hands.

Sam dug her in the ribs. "What's the matter?" he whispered. "You okay?"

Instead of replying, Hannah raised her face and thrust the notebook toward him. She saw his eyes flicker over her own work, then open wider when he came to what was underneath.

"What is this?"

She opened her mouth but didn't trust herself to speak.

"Hey! What's the matter? Why are you upset?" he mouthed. "It's only . . ." He stopped. He peered closer at the old-fashioned lettering, then back to her stricken face, then, for longer this time, at the page. She heard him catch his breath. "Hannah?" he said softly. "Who wrote this?"

Sam hardly ever used her name when talking to her. The fact that he did so now was a sign that he knew something was wrong. Very wrong. Suddenly the image of those magnetic letters sprang before her eyes, and a horrible connection began to form in her brain. She stared at him in panic.

"Come on," he muttered, getting up and grabbing her elbow with one hand and the notebook with the other. "Let's get out of here."

He shepherded her out of the library, along the corridor, and into an empty classroom. Then he drew up two chairs, and they sat down facing each other.

"It was her, Sam. Maisie wrote it!" Hannah blurted, her voice overloud now that whispering was no longer necessary.

For once he didn't contradict her, but held the book in his lap and stared soberly at the page. "What does it mean?"

"I don't know, but there was something a bit like it last night, only I tried to tell myself it had nothing to do with Maisie." She told him about the magnetic letters.

"Help me. Let me go," he muttered. "Is that all?"

She nodded. Then she caught her breath. "No! I've just remembered! On Sunday night, when I went out to the kitchen, four of the letters were grouped together. H-A-N-A. Like someone had been trying to write my name but couldn't spell properly."

"Mmm . . . guess that one could have been just coincidence?"

"That's what I thought then. But there's something else I haven't told you about. Like with those magnetic letters, I've been trying to explain it rationally, but I . . . I think, now, it's all connected." Then she told him about the smashed pitcher and the jar, the odd electrical outages, and the rapidly deteriorating state of the upstairs part of the house.

"Are you saying it's Maisie doing all this? Pulling radiators off walls? Damaging tiles and wallpaper?"

"I don't know," Hannah muttered. Put like that, it sounded ridiculous.

"Have the dreams stopped now?"

"They seem to have."

"And these messages? When was the first one?"

"Sunday night."

He frowned. "Why?"

"What do you mean, why?"

"Why *then*? You've been living in that house over a month. Then suddenly you get three weird messages in the space of four days. There must be a reason."

She stared at him. He seemed to be trying to apply logic to something that was essentially illogical.

"Think back," he said sharply. "I left you on Saturday afternoon. What happened between then and Sunday evening?"

"Nothing. At least, nothing important. On Sunday morning I did some work, and then we went out for lunch. In the afternoon I did some more work. It was after that, when I went out to the kitchen to make tea, that I saw the letters on the refrigerator."

"And that's all?"

"Yes, I think so. No . . . wait. There is something else. On Saturday evening, after you'd left, I did some drawing."

"What did you draw?"

She looked at him curiously. "It wasn't a real drawing. I was just copying that photo of Maisie. Trying to see if I could catch her expression."

"You *drew* her?"

"Well, yes." She suddenly felt alarmed. Why was Sam looking at her like that? "It wasn't anything special. Just a pencil sketch."

"I seem to remember it was just a pencil sketch that caused all the trouble last time." His voice was quiet, but he was looking at her intently, and she knew he was referring back to two Christmases ago, when she'd drawn the statues in the cathedral.

"That was different! Then I had no idea what I was doing. It was like something—or someone—took me over. Whatever it was was much bigger and more powerful than me. I was just kind of a . . . a channel. You know that."

"Maybe. But *you* were the one who was chosen to be the channel, remember. And it made something happen, didn't it? All the weird stuff that came later was triggered by *your drawing*."

"But this was nothing like that! I just chose Maisie as a subject. I was bored and looking for something to do!"

Sam stared at the floor for a few moments. Then he looked up. "Well, whatever the reason, it looks as though last Saturday night, you may have just accidentally drawn that girl into your life."

Hannah couldn't speak. She wanted to deny it, but then her eye fell once more on the notebook with the letters standing out in horrible clarity.

Suddenly he sat up straight. "Listen. Unless you get her exorcised, which has always seemed to me a pretty stupid kind of thing to do, you've got only one choice."

"What?"

"You've got to try to help her, like she's asked."

"But how? I don't even know what she wants me to do. All I've got is a lot of unconnected clues. And anyway, we don't even know if they really are all clues. Dad said he was paying far less for that house than he'd have expected. Maybe it was always in a bad state, and the real estate agency just did a quick cover-up job before renting it."

"Maybe. Or it's all part of a pattern." He frowned. "It could be that we just don't have all the right parts yet. There could be more to come."

Hannah shuddered, fervently hoping he was wrong. "You don't have to live there!"

He looked at her. "You think all this has something to do with that doll? If and when the aunt stuck the pins in that image, do you suppose she put a curse on Maisie, and somehow that curse is still there, a hundred and forty years later? Do you think she's asking you to help her to get rid of it?"

Hannah leaned her elbows on the desk and put her head in her hands. "It seems crazy. Unbelievable. But yes. I suppose that is what I think."

"Well, who do we know who can tell us something about curses and spells and stuff like that?"

"You mean—Mad Millie Murdoch?"

"Exactly! She helped us last time, didn't she?"

"But she retired more than a year ago. I don't even know if she's living at the same address. And for all we know, she might have given up all that kind of thing now."

"Then we'll find out. As soon as school's finished. Okay? And now, if you don't mind, we'll go back to the library."

He got up, and Hannah followed him to the door. She had no idea if Miss Murdoch would be any use, but even if she wasn't, there was something very comforting about having Sam on the case.

AT HOME WITH
THE FALLONS

DESPITE MISS MURDOCH HAVING retired from teaching math at Manningham, the school still had her telephone number, and when Hannah called it at three thirty that afternoon, she answered at once, sounding surprised but pleased to hear from her former student and inviting both Hannah and Sam over to her house at five o'clock.

"Good," said Sam. "That gives us an hour and a half. We'll go back to my place first."

The Fallons lived near the station, in a run-down development in a part of the city well known to the police for being a trouble spot. Once, Mr. Fallon's activities had made a lively contribution to this reputation, but for the past eighteen months he had lived a blameless life working as a mechanic at a nearby garage—which was why, when Sam and Hannah reached the apartment, only his mother and the twins were at home.

"Hannah, my love! What a treat!" exclaimed Mrs. Fallon. "You've come for tea? Why didn't you tell me, Sam? I'd've got something special in!"

Hannah started to say that she really hadn't come for tea and please not to go to any trouble on her account, but Eve Fallon was already in the tiny kitchen, clattering busily.

"Leave her alone." Sam grinned. "You know she loves it when you come."

Since she also knew from experience that Eve would refuse all offers of help, Hannah sat down on a sofa, noticing her own portrait of Sam, proudly displayed where a large gilt mirror had once hung. She smiled at seven-year-old Jack and Jessie, who were playing a computer game on the TV. "Hi! What's the game?"

They didn't reply, only smiling back shyly before scuttling off to their own room and leaving Hannah to wonder, not for the first time, how two such self-effacing children could possibly have been born into the same family as Sam Fallon.

He now picked up the remote control, switched to a TV program, and settled down beside her.

For the first time since that afternoon's chilling discovery, Hannah felt herself relax. She knew that if Mom were here, she would probably raise her eyebrows at the bright yellow wallpaper with its cheerful border of sunflowers, and she'd certainly consider the co-ordinating sunflower-strewn curtains way over the top, but as usual there was something reassuring about the warm, overfurnished room, whose sparkling cleanliness even Steph couldn't have found fault with. And today, thought Hannah, watching Sam idly flicking through the TV channels, it had something still more welcome. The little apartment was exactly what it appeared to be. It held no lurking surprises. Above all, it had no history. For an hour or so, she could push the image of that spidery writing to the back of her mind and retreat into the secure, furniture-spray-scented Fallon world.

Tea consisted, as usual, of all the deliciously unhealthy stuff Hannah was never allowed at home, and Hannah was soon contentedly munching peanut butter sandwiches and chocolate brownies, washed down with plenty of lemonade.

"We're going out later," said Sam with his mouth full.

"Oh. Where to?"

"Millie Murdoch's."

Eve looked suspicious. "I thought she'd retired."

"She has." Sam swallowed and licked his lips. "That's why we're going to see her. She's lonely, see. Doesn't get many visitors. We thought we'd go see her and cheer her up."

Hannah made an effort not to choke on her cake. The idea of Sam cheering up Miss Murdoch was entertaining. Driving her up a wall had been more like it.

His mother also looked unconvinced. "Why do you want to go bothering the poor old girl just when she's enjoying some peace at last? I'd have thought she'd had enough of you to last her a lifetime, Sam Fallon!"

Hannah thought so too, but it seemed unfair to leave him to do all the explaining. "I called her this afternoon, and she invited us to go there at five. She's expecting us." This at least was true, if misleading.

"Oh, well, if *you* spoke to her, I daresay it's fine." Eve nodded approvingly. "Just make sure he behaves himself." She followed this with a warning look at Sam and got up to clear the plates away.

Sam glanced at the cuckoo clock on the wall. "Four thirty. We'd better go. We might have to wait for a bus."

seventeen

A WITCH ADVISES

Eighty-two Martindale Road was just as Hannah remembered it. The front path divided a well-kept lawn, and the dark-blue paint on the front door matched velvet curtains neatly tied back to frame a ground-floor bay window, with only the flowers in the window boxes different from last time—where then there had been winter pansies, now there were scarlet geraniums. Everything about the house suggested quiet good taste. It was hard to believe that as well as being an ex–math teacher, Millicent Murdoch was also a witch.

Or, to be more precise, a Wiccan witch. Miss Murdoch had been anxious to make this distinction clear to Hannah on her previous visit, but as far Hannah had been able to tell, it just meant that Mad

Millie didn't ride around the countryside on a broom-stick, laying curses on people's cattle. She had, however, bravely come to their rescue eighteen months ago, and despite her nickname, beneath the witchery lay an unexpected store of old-fashioned common sense.

Miss Murdoch opened the door and beamed out at them. The long, pink-tipped nose and receding chin still lent her a slightly mouselike appearance, but her gray hair, which before had been drawn back and fas-tened insecurely, was now cut short and framed her narrow face as tidily as the dark-blue curtains framed her windows.

"Come in, come in! How very good to see you both!"

She led them into a gleaming, modern kitchen and told them to sit down at the table, which held a bottle and three glasses.

"I hope you will try some of my homemade elder-flower cordial," she said brightly. "I always find it so refreshing on a hot day, and really, the weather has been very good lately, hasn't it? Or are you finding it too warm for your examinations? They are this week, aren't they? And you must tell me all about your stud-ies. How are you getting on in mathematics, Hannah?"

"Not too badly, thanks, Miss Murdoch." In fact, Hannah had been getting on slightly better since Miss

Murdoch had stopped teaching her, but it would, of course, have been tactless to mention it.

"And you, Sam? I seem to remember that you were always one of my brightest students."

Sam gave her a sickly smile, and Hannah decided it was time to change the subject. It didn't seem right to launch straight into what they'd really come to talk about, so she tried out a little polite conversation first. "Are you enjoying your retirement, Miss Murdoch?"

"Yes, thank you, my dear. I have joined one or two clubs, which keep me busy in the evenings, and last year I started to grow my own vegetables. My cauliflowers have been much admired. Some have even won prizes at the local gardening club!"

"Well . . . that's nice." Hannah smiled.

"Indeed, and it has put me in touch with some very interesting people. I have spent many a pleasant evening discussing the merits of various methods of planting and propagation, usually over a cup of herbal tea, or, occasionally"—here Millie looked mischievously daring—"enlivened by a glass of something more intoxicating!"

Hannah did her best to return a conspiratorial smile but was prevented by a sharp kick on the shin from Sam, who seemed to think it was time to cut out the chat and get to the point. She retaliated by kicking him back, then coughed nervously.

"Actually, Miss Murdoch, we're here . . . that is, Sam and I have come to ask your advice about something."

"Of course," replied their hostess, smiling graciously. "What can I do for you? Don't tell me you have taken up gardening!"

"We've taken up witch hunting," said Sam.

The smile left Miss Murdoch's face abruptly.

"Well, ghost hunting, really," said Hannah.

"I see." She sighed. "I had a suspicion that this might not be a purely social call. You had better tell me what is going on."

So Hannah took a deep breath and told Miss Murdoch about moving temporarily into Cowleigh Lodge. She told her about the dreams, and the book of fairy tales, and the doll they had found. She recounted, as accurately as she could, the relevant bits of what Mrs. Grocott and her daughter had said. Lastly, she told her about the drawing of Maisie, and the subsequent odd happenings, including the messages, the last of which had appeared that afternoon.

"Mmm," said Miss Murdoch when Hannah seemed to have finished. She pursed her lips and looked thoughtful. "It sounds remarkably like attention seeking to me."

"Maisie, you mean?"

"Yes. Breakages, electrical interference, minor damage. All are known signs of spirit activity."

"But why? What does she want us to do?"

"Help her. Let her go. Isn't that what the messages said?" Millie sat back in her chair and rested her hands on the kitchen table, lightly drumming her fingers. Then she looked up. When she spoke again, her voice was brisk, businesslike.

"As I understand it, the two of you suspect this aunt of doing away with her niece by means of witchcraft."

"All the evidence points that way," said Sam.

"Evidence?" Miss Murdoch's voice was sharp. "A few dreams, a child's book, and a little half-remembered servants' gossip? Hardly evidence, I should have thought!"

"There's the doll as well," Hannah reminded her.

"Ah, yes. The doll," mused Millie. "The doll that has been altered so that it looks like Maisie and that appears to have been stuck with pins." She frowned and shook her head slowly. "It all seems rather . . . *amateurish.*" She might have been passing judgment on an inferior cauliflower.

"But it worked, didn't it?" insisted Hannah. "Maisie died!"

"So did a great many other Victorian children, unfortunately. The fact that you have no strictly rational explanation for her death doesn't necessarily mean that there wasn't one."

"So why is she asking for help, if she died naturally?"

"I said that there might be a rational explanation. That would not preclude the possibility of an unnatural death."

Hannah looked mystified, but Sam's eyes glittered. "You mean she could have been poisoned?"

"Think about it. If this woman really had sole charge of her little niece while she was confined to her bed, she would hardly have needed to resort to witchcraft in order to do her harm. In those days, many poisons were readily available over a pharmacist's counter to those who could prove a legitimate reason for needing them. Arsenic, for example, was commonly used to fatten pigs and poultry. It can be added in small quantities to a patient's food or drink over a long period of time without too much risk of discovery. To begin with, it causes headaches, drowsiness, some confusion, perhaps—not so very different from a feverish illness, and the symptoms can be easily explained as such. But then, little by little, the effects accumulate, you see. Eventually, of course, it will be fatal. Yes . . ." Miss Murdoch nodded thoughtfully. "In her position, I think I should probably have chosen arsenic."

Hannah began to think that this had gone far enough. "But *why* would she do it? What motive did she have for killing Maisie?"

Millie looked offended. "How on earth should I know? I was merely attempting a hypothesis."

"It doesn't help us anyway," said Sam flatly. "We can't prove anything after all this time."

"And that means we can't help Maisie," muttered Hannah.

"Do you think that is what she wants? For you to discover how she died?" asked Miss Murdoch.

"It would be a start, I suppose," Hannah said dejectedly.

Millie didn't reply.

After a moment or so, Hannah looked at her watch. "We should go." She stood up. "Thanks, Miss Murdoch. I'm sorry we bothered you with all this."

"Not at all. You asked for my advice. Just at the moment, my advice is to get rid of that doll."

"What?" Hannah stared at her. "But . . . you said you didn't think that was what caused Maisie's death!"

"Frankly, I don't. Nevertheless, it is an unpleasant object to have in one's home, and I cannot believe it is helping the situation." Millie stood up and walked with them to the front door.

But as Sam went out, Miss Murdoch drew Hannah back. "I am glad that you have Sam with you in this," she said quietly. "You need him. However, don't forget: It is *your* attention that this child seems to want. It is *your* help she has asked for. Perhaps you should begin by asking yourself what only *you* can do for her."

eighteen

THE BOX

"At least she took us seriously," said Sam as soon as they were both outside the front door. "She could have just told us to go home and forget all about it."

"I suppose so." In some ways, Miss Murdoch's matter-of-fact acceptance of the situation was what had alarmed Hannah most.

"She wasn't much help, though," he went on. "Like I said, even if she's right about the poison, we've no way of proving it. Not without an exhumation order, and you need special permission for one of those."

"How come you know so much about it?"

"Police dramas. They're always digging people up and finding they're stuffed full of poison."

"Ah."

"Are you okay?"

"Not really. How am I going to get rid of that doll?"

"Burn it."

"In the middle of summer? You think I'm going to light a bonfire without anybody noticing?"

"Put it in the garbage, then."

"They don't collect until next Monday."

"Well, bury it! Take it to a dump somewhere! What does it matter how you do it, just so long as you get it out of your life?"

"All right, I'll think of something." She sighed gloomily. "And now I'd better get home and find out what's happened while I've been out. The rate things are going, the house could have fallen down by now."

Cowleigh Lodge was still standing, however, and when Hannah let herself in at six thirty that evening, her mother's face told her that nothing too disastrous had gone on while she was at school. In fact, Mom was looking quite excited about something.

"You remember I showed you the carpet in my room—how it wasn't tacked down anymore near the window? Well, today I was up there sorting out some boxes, and I saw that it had come completely loose from the floor in one corner and a bit of it was folded over. The draft from the window must have done it, I suppose. Anyway, I'd just bent down to put it back when I noticed that one of the floorboards is sawed off, about a foot from the window, and the spare bit wasn't lying quite straight. So I picked it up to put it back properly, and guess what I found underneath?"

Hannah held her breath. She wasn't sure she wanted to know.

"This!" Mom reached behind her and picked up something from the kitchen counter.

It was a square wooden box, about eight inches across, the lid inlaid with ivory.

"Pretty, isn't it?" said Mom. "Open it. It's not locked."

Hannah raised the lid, noticing that on the inside of it someone had carefully inscribed the initials L.H. in black ink. There were three things in the box: a small, folded, embroidered handkerchief; a little oval gold locket on a fine chain; and another, smaller box made of papier-mâché. Hannah lifted this out first. The lid wasn't hinged, but it was shaped to fit tightly and needed a lot of coaxing before it eventually shot off, discharging what looked like about half a dozen tiny whitish-brown pebbles, which rolled onto the floor.

Hannah bent down to pick them up. "What are they?" she asked, mystified.

Her mother peered closely, then laughed. "Teeth!"

"Teeth? Ugh!" Hastily Hannah dropped the little

collection on the counter. "How horrible!"

"Not horrible, just sentimental. They're baby teeth. I've kept the first ones you lost too." Mom scooped up the tiny relics and replaced them in their box as Hannah picked up the locket.

"Does this open?"

"Maybe. I didn't look. Oh, yes. See, there's a clasp on the side." Her mother took the locket from her and gently flipped up the tiny gold clasp to reveal, on one side, a few strands of dark brown hair twisted into a neat loop, and on the other, the painted miniature of a small child. "And this, if I'm not mistaken, is the owner of the teeth. What do you think?"

Hannah didn't reply. Instead she picked up the handkerchief. Carefully she unfolded it. The linen was stiff, the delicate border of leaves and flowers stained with age. But it was something else that held Hannah's attention.

Diagonally within the border, picked out in neat, cursively looped stitching of cornflower blue, were four evenly spaced lines.

To Dearest Mama
From your Loving
Daughter Maisie
Aged 9 years and 2 months

"How nice," commented Mom, smiling. "And what beautiful sewing! She would have been taught to add her exact age to work like this to show the standard she'd reached by that time. Mind you, I suspect she had a certain amount of help with this. It's pretty impressive for a nine-year-old!"

"The colors haven't faded, either," murmured Hannah. "This blue is still quite solid."

"Colors only fade when they're exposed to light. This was probably kept folded in a drawer until it found its way under the floorboards. Goodness knows how it got there. It seems an odd place for a mother to keep her precious little collection—hidden away like that."

"It might not have been her that put it there."

"No? I suppose not. Anyway." Mom began replacing the contents of the box. "What shall we do with it now that we've found it?"

Hannah glanced at the refrigerator. The magnetic letters were still crowded together as she'd left them last night. There was no new message. And yet the finding of the box was significant, she felt sure. Or else why had that corner of carpet been so conveniently turned up? She thought of the wallpaper, the bathroom tiles, the loose screws, the fireplace board. Suddenly she had the bizarre notion that the house was *undressing*.

Little by little, it was shedding its bland modern coat to reveal . . . what? Disconnected glimpses into a long-dead world? Or was there, like Sam had said, some pattern—some logical progression to a series of clues that she hadn't yet understood?

She shivered. Then she turned back to Mom. "You choose. It doesn't matter."

That night she lay awake for a long time, worrying about the doll. How to get rid of it? And when? But she couldn't think properly because her brain kept bombarding her with odd fragments of half-remembered speech. Miss Murdoch's voice: *"In her position, I think I should probably have chosen arsenic."* Sam's: *"They're always digging people up and finding they're stuffed full of poison."* And something Emily had started to tell her, weeks ago . . . something that, for some odd reason, made her think of that little locket. At last she fell asleep.

When she woke, it wasn't quite six o'clock, but the sky was already bright outside and her brain felt clear, as if the jumbled thoughts of last night had miraculously ordered themselves while she slept.

Now, suddenly, she knew what to do.

PASSING THE PARCEL

SHE DRESSED QUICKLY AND ran downstairs. The screwdriver was lying on top of the toolbox, where she'd put it after fixing the shelf. Back on the landing, she loosened the screws holding the board that covered the entrance to the loft and moved it carefully to one side. Sam hadn't quite closed the door behind it, so there was no need for the wire coat hanger—she simply pulled the door toward her. Then, with her heart beating uncomfortably fast, she ascended the stairs.

But whatever she'd expected to find, the attic room was just as she and Sam had left it—the dust thick and undisturbed save for their own footprints of almost three weeks ago, the windowsill with the same dead flies. And just inside the door, sprawled unnaturally like the victim of a road accident, lay the doll.

Hannah seized it and ran back down the stairs. On the landing she closed the brown door as quietly as possible, replaced the screws in the board, and went down to the kitchen, where she laid the doll on the table. Then she went into the living room, opened a drawer in the desk, took out a pad of paper, and after a few moments' thought wrote a short letter. She put it in an envelope, printed a name on the front, and went back into the kitchen. In the cupboard under the sink she found a pile of newspapers and a plastic shopping bag. In another drawer she found tape.

The little wooden box was still on the counter where Mom had left it last night. Opening it, she took out the locket and hung it around the doll's neck.

Now for the worst part. With trembling fingers, she grabbed three sheets of newspaper and wrapped the doll tightly, winding the tape around and around. She repeated the process with another three sheets, then more sheets, until the parcel became a bulky, shapeless mass, like the ones in the game she used to play at parties as a very young child. Only this was no game, she reminded herself grimly. The thing beneath those layers was no pretty toy.

Finally she bundled the parcel into the plastic shopping bag, taped the letter to the outside, and scribbled a note to her mother to say she'd gone to school early to look over a few things in a textbook she'd left in her desk. Then she let herself out of the house and walked quickly through the still-quiet streets until she reached the main city precinct and the imposing nineteenth-century building that was the Carlyle Street police station.

"I'd like to speak to Detective Sergeant Bean, please," she told the man behind the reception desk.

"Detective *Inspector* Bean," said the policeman reprovingly. "And what might that be concerning, young lady?"

"Sorry," she said, reddening. "I didn't know he'd been promoted. I need to give him something. It's very important."

"Oh, yes? So important that you can't tell me what he's likely to expect?" The man looked suspiciously at the shopping bag.

"No. That is, I'd rather give it to him myself, if you don't mind. He knows me," she added hopefully.

"He does, does he? Might that be socially or, shall we say, professionally?"

"Professionally," she replied with dignity.

"Is that so? Name, please." He yawned and pulled a pad of paper toward him.

"Hannah Price."

The policeman's eyebrows shot up. "Hannah Price?

Are you the one who helped to recover that piece of property from the cathedral the year before last?"

Hannah nodded modestly, though it would have been more true to say that it was she and Sam who had recovered it, and the police who had helped.

"Well! Why didn't you say so before?" The man pushed the paper away, his manner suddenly becoming friendly and cooperative. "Now don't you worry, Miss Price. I'm afraid Inspector Bean isn't in the office just yet, but as soon as he is, I'll make sure he gets this."

"Thank you." Hannah turned and left the station, feeling as though the worst part of the day was already over. Now she only had exams to worry about.

twenty

CHANGE IN THE WEATHER

"I DON'T BELIEVE IT!" Sam stared at her. They were standing in a corner of the playground at lunchtime. "You took that thing to the police and asked them to do an *autops*y? Are you crazy?"

"Maybe. It was Millie Murdoch who gave me the idea, you see. When she said that if she'd had a choice, and wanted to poison someone without being detected, she'd have chosen arsenic."

"So? She was just guessing."

"And afterward, you said all that about the police digging up bodies and searching for poison."

"Yes?" He still looked utterly baffled.

"Then I remembered something else. It was that day in the library, when we were studying, and Emily had lost a page of notes on the death of Napoleon.

The bell had just rung and I was trying to get away, but she was going on about what she'd found out on the internet."

"Typical."

"Yes, well. Anyway, she was saying that toward the end of his life, while he was in exile, Bonaparte got the idea that someone was trying to poison him. Nothing was ever proved, but years later, some of his hair was analyzed and found to contain arsenic."

Sam raised his eyebrows, but this time he kept quiet.

"So I got to thinking. If it's possible to detect arsenic in a person's hair long after they've died, then it must be possible to detect other things as well. So I thought, If only we had some of Maisie's hair, cut off not too long before she died, we might have a chance to find out what she died *of*. Do you see?"

"No." He frowned. "At least, I understand what you mean, but . . . we don't have any of her hair. Unfortunately."

"Oh, yes, we do!" she said softly. "And what's more, we've had it all the time!"

Suddenly the penny dropped. He gasped. "The doll! You mean . . . that wig? It's real hair?"

Hannah nodded.

Sam's eyes sparkled excitedly. Then his face fell.

He frowned. "How do we know it's hers, though? It could be anybody's. Her mother's. A complete stranger's."

For the first time, Hannah allowed herself a small, triumphant smile. "It just so happens that we have another sample. I gave that to the police too." And she told him about the contents of the little wooden box.

It wasn't often that Sam gave her a look of whole-hearted admiration, but this was one of those times, and for a few moments she basked.

The moment was short-lived, however.

"It won't work, you know." He shook his head regretfully.

"What?"

"All this. Don't get me wrong, I think it's brilliant what you've figured out. But it's too neat. Too . . . perfect. In real life, kids don't really get to deduce answers from far-fetched clues like this and have themselves proved right. That's the trouble with police dramas. They're not real life."

Hannah bit her lip. She felt as if she'd brought him a nice fat balloon and he'd rewarded her by sticking a pin in it. But what really hurt was that she knew he was right. It had seemed like such a great idea at the time that she hadn't stopped to think about just how ridiculous her request would sound to a policeman, even a sympathetic one like Sergeant—or rather, Inspector—Bean. "Oh, well." She sighed philosophically. "There's one good thing, anyway. At least we've gotten rid of that horrible doll."

"True." He grinned. "That'll be something to cheer you up when you get arrested for wasting police time!"

⇥⇥⇥

For the past few weeks, the weather had been getting steadily hotter. The temperature was still rising, but the sky had lost its bright clarity and the air was close. There was talk of storms on the way.

"I hope it stays dry for Saturday," said Sam, frowning, as they left school that afternoon.

"Why? What's happening on Saturday?"

"The fair's this weekend, dummy! You're coming, aren't you?"

"Oh. Yes. I guess so."

The Midsummer Fair was a highlight of the city calendar, drawing large crowds of tourists as well as most of the local population. Usually Hannah looked forward to it as much as anyone, but recently she'd had other things on her mind.

"The forecast says it should be okay, just, but they've been wrong before."

Hannah chuckled. The only other time Sam took the faintest interest in the weather forecast was before a football match. "Don't worry. If it's too bad, we can always go back to my house. It's only half a mile from the common."

She left him at the school gates and trudged home, wondering anxiously what might be waiting for her this time. But for once, there were no new developments, and her mother seemed, if not exactly cheerful, at least calm that evening. Toby was still missing, but apart from that, things seemed normal enough.

Except that when Hannah went to bed that night, the atmosphere seemed even more oppressive. She opened the window as wide as it would go, but it made no difference to the air inside the room, which stayed humid and stifling. There was something about the damp atmosphere that made her uneasy, and that night, Hannah fought sleep. It wasn't until nearly four that she at last gave in, and then she slept deeply, waking three hours later to the noise of the alarm and a splitting headache.

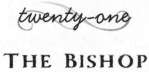

THE BISHOP

NOT SURPRISINGLY, HANNAH WASN'T at her brightest in school the following day. The first exam was math—a subject that gave her a headache at the best of times, let alone after a bad night—and by the end of the morning she felt as though someone were attacking her with a mallet.

"What's the matter with you?" demanded Sam, seeing her sitting with her elbows on the desk, her head clasped tightly in her hands, and a look of pain on her face. "It wasn't that bad, was it?"

"Actually," muttered Hannah, from between gritted teeth, "it was. But that's beside the point. I've got the worst headache ever."

"Why don't you go and see the nurse?"

She nodded, then wished she hadn't, as it set off

the mallet once more. After a few seconds she stood up and walked slowly out of the classroom.

But when she got to the nurse's office, it was already occupied by somebody else. Henry Knight was sitting on a chair, in tears, while Mrs. Jennings, the school nurse, held the telephone receiver and tapped her foot impatiently.

Hannah withdrew and waited outside until, after a couple of minutes, she heard the receiver being put down, and a moment or so later the nurse appeared with Henry, leading him to another room on the other side of the corridor.

"You wait here," Hannah heard her say kindly. "As soon as I can get hold of your mother, I'll let you know." Coming back out, she noticed Hannah. "Sorry, were you waiting for me?"

"Sort of. What's wrong with Henry?"

"Don't ask!" She shook her head. "I just wish I could reach his parents. I've been trying his mother's contact number for the last hour!"

Suddenly she noticed Hannah's pale face, and it seemed to dawn on her that here was another patient. "What's the matter with you, more like! Do you feel ill?"

"I'm okay. Just a headache."

"Exam this afternoon?"

"Yes."

Mrs. Jennings nodded sympathetically. She disappeared and returned a few moments later with a cloth soaked in cold water. "Go and lie down for half an hour with this on your forehead. You'll miss lunch, but I'll wake you in time to grab a sandwich from the cafeteria."

Hannah took the compress gratefully and allowed herself to be led into a small room with a narrow bed. Mrs. Jennings closed the curtains and left her to sleep.

❧

It was fortunate that the very last exam of all was art—not only because, in spite of her headache and an almost sleepless night, even Hannah knew that in this one subject she really didn't have to try too hard to do well, but mainly because for two blissful hours, she was able to forget all about Maisie Holt.

But by three o'clock that afternoon, the respite was over. Exams had officially finished, and although there were still a few more days of the term left, most people were acting as if the holidays had already started. The noise in the entrance hall was deafening.

To Hannah, it was all too much. Drawing, even under exam conditions, took her over so completely that it always left her feeling drained, and now, still nursing the remains of the headache, she just wanted to escape. The trouble was, she didn't feel like going back to Cowleigh Lodge. Last night might not have thrown up any more alarming revelations, but there had been something suffocating about the atmosphere that made her unwilling to return straightaway. Where else, then?

After a few moments' thought, she knew the answer. Leaving the school by the main door, she crossed the playground and walked down Tanners' Lane until she reached the high wall that separated the lane from the cathedral on the north side. At the far end of it, she turned onto a wide gravel path, which led to the main door at the west end of the cathedral. A large litter bin stood to one side of the path, but there were still a few candy bar wrappers and empty drink cans on the gravel, and as she pushed open the door, she noticed that the shop just outside was crowded with people buying postcards and little plaster models.

Once inside, she breathed in deeply, relishing the familiar smell of old wood and stone and melted candle wax that made up the special atmosphere of the ancient building. Slowly she walked down the long north aisle until she reached the statues of the Virgin and Child that were the originals of the plaster models being sold outside and sat down in a pew beside them.

Six hundred years ago, a man called Jacob

Martin had carved the statues from a single piece of oak. But for some reason he hadn't joined them. They were individuals, the Child able to be separated from the Mother, just like a real baby, and it was this baby that, the Christmas before last, had mysteriously disappeared.

Since then, Hannah had returned to the cathedral from time to time to see the reunited couple, partly with a sense of pride that it had been she and Sam who had made it possible, but mostly because there was something about the statues that drew her back. Something calming. Like visiting old friends.

She had been sitting there for about ten minutes before she noticed a large figure approaching down the north aisle. He wore an open-necked cotton shirt, which he had wisely not attempted to tuck into the waistband of his light-colored summer trousers, in spite of the fact they were cut to a generous scale. If Hannah hadn't known better, she might have thought he had just wandered in off the street in search of a cool place to sit. As it was, she gave him a happy smile of recognition, and the bishop eased himself into the pew next to her.

"Thought I saw you up here," he said, returning her smile. "I'm not interrupting anything, am I?" He indicated the statues with a nod.

"No," replied Hannah. "I was just sitting."

"Ah." The bishop seemed to accept this as a perfectly natural explanation, and for a while they sat together in companionable silence. For it had been through the theft of the statue that they had gotten to know each other, and its recovery had laid its own special seal on their friendship.

Then she became aware that he was eyeing her thoughtfully. "You're looking pale. Anything the matter?"

"I just had a bad night. It gave me a headache."

"Bad luck." He frowned. "Problems?"

"No." She hesitated. "Not exactly."

"In my experience, that means yes," he said briskly. "Why don't we go outside? These pews are far too uncomfortable for someone of my size."

He led her out through a side door in the south wall to a secluded spot where there was a shaded bench. "Wait here a minute."

She watched him walk over to a little booth selling cold drinks and snacks. Five minutes later he was back, carrying two double-scoop ice-cream cones. He handed one to Hannah. "We're a little more commercial since that business the Christmas before last," he said, sighing regretfully. "But it would seem churlish not to take advantage of it once in a while."

"Thank you." She took the ice cream, and he settled himself comfortably beside her.

"Well?"

She shook her head. "It would take too long to explain."

He looked at his watch. "In twenty-five minutes' time, I have a meeting in the chapter house. Until then, I'm all yours. That is, if you want to tell me."

Again she hesitated. It had been one thing to tell the story to Miss Murdoch—Hannah already knew that she believed in a world where such things could happen. But the bishop was different. She had no idea how he might react. He had offered his time, however, and it seemed rude to refuse. So she took a deep breath and plunged in.

"It started with this dream I had."

At first she tried to simplify the facts by leaving bits out, but soon she found it impossible to explain properly without including all the details—the nightmares, the book, the doll, the testimony of Mrs. Grocott and her daughter, the drawing of Maisie, the messages, and the rapidly deteriorating state of Cowleigh Lodge, with its accompanying electrical failures. The only thing she didn't confess to was the delivery of the doll to Inspector Bean. She already felt embarrassed enough about that.

But the bishop was a good listener, as she had discovered once before, and other than taking the occasional absentminded lick of his ice cream, he gave her his undivided attention. By the time she had finished talking, he was looking distinctly unhappy.

"This house," he began. "The move will have been stressful for you, especially during exams and so on. And it's not unusual to find difficulties with sleeping in a strange environment. Do you think that perhaps . . . ?"

"No," said Hannah. "I'm sorry, but I'm not imagining all this. Really."

"Forgive me." He shook his head apologetically. "I don't mean to seem patronizing, but has anyone else witnessed these, um, phenomena?"

"That depends on what you mean by phenomena. My mother's noticed the damage to the house, the weird electrical stuff. And Sam saw the third message. The one in my notebook."

"Have you told anyone at school about this?" he asked sharply.

She shook her head. "No. That message couldn't have been written by anyone there, if that's what you mean."

The bishop sighed. Then he sat up straight and seemed to change tack. "Let us suppose, for the sake of hypothesis, that the child really is seeking your help. What does she want from you? To discover how she died?"

Hannah looked at him. Was he taking her seriously at last? She couldn't tell, but this was very like the question Miss Murdoch had asked, and she gave him much the same reply. "Yes. I think that has to be what she wants. It fits with all the things we've discovered."

"And just supposing, again for the sake of hypothesis, that you were somehow able to obtain proof that this aunt deliberately set out to kill her little niece. How would you feel about that?"

"How would *I* feel? I . . . I'm not sure. It's Maisie who matters, isn't it?"

"Maisie is dead," he said gently. "She has been dead for more than a hundred years. How can you help her now?"

"But she's asking me to. I can't just ignore her."

"No? Perhaps not." The bishop rubbed his chin. "I could pray with you, if you would like?"

Hannah squirmed uncomfortably. "No. Thank you. I'm sorry. I . . . don't think I could handle that."

"Oh, well. I daresay I shall have to handle it on my own, then." The bishop didn't look particularly disappointed. "Just now, I interrupted something private

153

in there, didn't I?" He indicated the cathedral behind them.

"The statues? Not really. It's just that I go and sit there sometimes. It feels kind of . . ."

"Helpful?"

"Yes. I'm not sure why, exactly."

"Then might I suggest that you return to them now?"

She took this as a dismissal and stood up.

"Incidentally, will you be going to the fair tomorrow?"

"Fair? Oh! I'd forgotten. It's Saturday tomorrow. Yes. I'm going with Sam."

"Good. It will be a chance for you to forget about all this business for a little while. Go and enjoy yourself! My wife and I are planning to put in an appearance, so maybe we will see you there, as long as the weather holds. I believe a storm is forecast later on. Oh, and by the way," he added a bit sheepishly, "if you happen to speak to my wife, I wonder if you would mind not mentioning the ice cream?"

"I won't say a word," she promised as she finished her cone.

The bishop winked, briefly enclosed both her hands in his own, and left.

Hannah went back inside the cathedral, partly to

delay the moment when she would have to go home, but also to spend a few last moments beside the Virgin and Child. There was nobody else nearby, and she still had them to herself. As she sat there quietly watching them, it struck her, not for the first time, that although the eyes of each were so firmly fixed on the other's, their gaze seemed at the same time to radiate outward. As though what they shared was so plentiful that it spilled over, casting lingering rays over all it touched, like the soft, honeyed light of a summer's evening.

twenty-two

UNEXPECTED EVIDENCE

THE INTENSE, MUGGY HEAT outside came as a shock after the cool interior of the cathedral, and Hannah trudged home slowly. To delay the moment of getting there a little further, she took the long way back to Cowleigh Lodge, the route that passed the church, and, on an impulse, pushed open the gate to the graveyard and walked in. The grass was newly mowed, its scent lying heavy on the still air, and a bumblebee moved placidly among the flowering shrubs that lined the path between the graves.

Hannah left the path and walked the short distance to the plain gray stone with its light covering of yellow lichen, and stared once more at the stark message.

MAISIE HOLT
BORN MARCH 4, 1866
DIED JUNE 23, 1877

But as before, it gave nothing back. She felt no shiver of apprehension, no sense of brooding presence. Maisie wasn't here, any more than any of these other people whose remains lay beneath the sweet-smelling turf. Wherever the dead were, it wasn't in this pleasant, well-kept garden.

Yet, after leaving the churchyard, as she walked home, something nagged her. The feeling took a little while to identify, but at last she remembered. It was the last line of the inscription on that stone.

DIED JUNE 23, 1877

Now it wasn't the year that struck her but the date. June 23. Tomorrow would be the anniversary of the day on which Maisie Holt had died.

When Hannah got back to Cowleigh Lodge, her mother was standing at the sink, running water over a tray of ice cubes. "Good day?" she inquired brightly. "How was math?"

"Horrible."

"You always say that!"

"That's because it's always horrible."

"D'you think you've passed?"

"Doubt it."

"Oh, well," said Mom philosophically. "Math isn't everything. Water?" She held out a glass.

"Thanks." Hannah gulped down a mouthful and took the glass into the living room. She sank down into a chair and despondently switched on her cell phone with the idea of calling Sam. There was one new voicemail. She pressed the button and listened. It was a man's voice—controlled and official sounding.

"This is Inspector Bean, hoping to speak to Miss Hannah Price. Would you call me back, please? Thank you."

Hannah's heart sank. That was all she needed after a bad day. The inspector was clearly calling to give her a good telling off for wasting his time. Why couldn't he just have ignored her stupid request? Oh, well, she thought miserably. Better get it over with. She pressed the keys and waited for the ringing tone.

"Hello?"

"Inspector Bean? It's Hannah. Hannah Price."

"Ah, yes. Thanks for returning my call."

Hannah immediately launched into a confused apology, not only for marching unannounced into the police station, but also for handing in an unsolicited parcel and generally wasting the inspector's valuable time by asking for two ridiculous tests that she knew couldn't possibly be any use, even if he'd had them carried out, which of course he hadn't, had he? She would have gone on even longer if he hadn't stopped her in midsentence.

"Calm down, Miss Price. No need to get so worked up. I've done what you asked."

"You have?" She almost dropped the phone in astonishment.

"That's right. It just so happened that your parcel arriving on my desk coincided with a visit from a mate of mine in forensics. He owed me a favor, and when I told him it was for a friend, he said he'd have a look at your little request when he had time." The inspector chuckled. "Couple of old family heirlooms, are they?"

"Not exactly."

"No? Well, anyway. To be honest, once I'd handed over the parcel, I forgot all about it. I never thought I'd get the results landing on my desk within forty-eight hours. We're lucky to get a response like that in a murder inquiry!"

"You mean he did the tests?"

"He did. And it's as you thought. The two samples are almost certainly from the same head, though the hair in the locket is finer. Probably taken when the subject was about two or three years old."

"I see. Well, thanks," she said awkwardly. "Listen, I'm really sorry to have put you both to so much trouble for nothing. It was a stupid idea, I know that now, and I should never have bothered you with it."

"But don't you want to know the results of the second test?" The inspector sounded puzzled. "You must have had some reason for suspecting something, shall we say . . . unusual, in the sample?"

"Oh, not really." She felt herself growing hot with embarrassment. "Like I said, it was just a stupid hunch."

"In that case," said the inspector drily, "it's an odd coincidence that your hunch turned out to be one hundred percent correct."

"Meaning . . . what?" Suddenly the heat left Hannah's face, and she clutched the phone hard, afraid she might drop it.

"Meaning that the hair shafts showed an unusually high concentration of arsenic, probably the result of prolonged exposure."

It was just as well that Hannah was already sitting down, because she suddenly felt decidedly wobbly.

"Was there . . . enough to kill someone?"

"More than likely, I should think."

"So the person this hair came from could have been . . ." She paused and swallowed hard. "Murdered?"

"Maybe. What's this all about, anyway? Some skeleton in the family cupboard?"

Hannah didn't reply. She was still in shock.

"Ah, well. It's water under the bridge now, isn't it? That doll's well over a hundred years old, I should say. By the way, there was one other thing. Those yellowish-brown marks. Apparently they're iodine. When I was a child, it used to be put on cuts and scrapes. Can't imagine why anyone would have wanted to paint it on a doll, but there you are. Kids do funny things to their toys, don't they? Anyhow." Inspector Bean cleared his throat. "To get back to the present, you specifically requested that, after analysis, the—ah—evidence should be destroyed."

"And?" Hannah held her breath.

"Oh, it's been destroyed all right." The inspector chuckled. "In fact, I've a feeling that's why you got your results so promptly. Nasty old thing, my colleague said. Apparently he couldn't wait to get rid of it!"

Hannah shivered. "Did he say how he'd . . . disposed of it?"

"Incinerated, I should imagine. With all the other trash."

Cremation, thought Hannah grimly. That should do it. She managed to pull herself together enough to thank him for going to so much trouble on her account, said good-bye, and put the phone down. After a few seconds she picked it up again and pressed Sam's number.

twenty-three

CAFÉ TALK

AN HOUR AND A half later, they were sitting at a table on the sidewalk outside a little café near the cathedral square, enjoying a glass of Sprite to celebrate the end of exams. At least, that was what they'd told their mothers. In reality, Sam was just recovering from the shock of hearing what Inspector Bean had had to say.

"So Millie was right! It was arsenic that killed her, after all!"

"Shh! Keep your voice down!" hissed Hannah as half a dozen interested faces turned toward them from the surrounding tables.

"But that's incredible," he muttered. "You know, I never thought . . ."

"Neither did I. Not really. Like you said, it was just

too fantastic to actually work in real life."

"But it did." He grinned. "Well, congratulations, Sherlock Price!"

"Thanks." Hannah smiled modestly.

"I suppose that's it, then?"

"What do you mean?"

"You've done it. Solved the problem. With luck, there won't be any more weird green dreams or magnetic messages, and all the radiators will stay attached to the walls." He took a swig from the glass in front of him and glared at the woman opposite, who had apparently been attempting to follow this bizarre conversation. She blushed and looked away.

"I hope you're right." Hannah sipped her own drink thoughtfully. "It's a pity we'll never know why she did it, though."

"Who? The aunt?" He shrugged. "Maybe she wanted their money. Maisie was an only child, wasn't she? With her out of the way, there was only Mrs. Holt left. For all we know, she was going to be the next victim."

Hannah nodded. "Maybe."

"What's the matter? If I'd solved something like this, I'd be dancing on the table!"

"Just as well you didn't, then," she said, glancing around at the other customers, who were now chatting quietly and enjoying the evening sunshine.

"You must be relieved, though?" he persisted.

"Yes. Yes, of course I am." She swirled the Sprite, watching the tiny bubbles cluster against the side of the glass.

"By the way," said Sam. "Nearly forgot. You missed a bit of drama after school this afternoon."

"Oh?"

"Henry Knight. Apparently when he got to school today, he had a black eye."

She groaned. "Oh, no. Not again! That must be why he was with Mrs. Jennings when I got there. So someone must have persuaded him to go and get some help at last?"

"As soon as his teacher saw the eye, she frog-marched him straight to the nurse's office."

"Good. About time too. Only . . . I'm sure Henry didn't have a black eye when I saw him." Hannah was puzzled.

"Exactly. Mrs. Jennings spotted the problem straightaway and cured it."

"How did she do that?"

"Eye makeup remover."

"*What?* You mean . . . it wasn't a real black eye?"

He shook his head. "It was a fake. The same as all those other bruises."

Hannah's eyes widened. "All this time, nobody suspected him?"

"Seems not."

"But wait a minute!" She frowned. "How do you know all this?"

"One of his friends overheard the principal talking to Mrs. Jennings in her office. It turns out that Henry was just trying to get his parents' attention by making it look like he was being bullied, only they were both too busy to notice. Apparently they never come to any school functions, and Henry gets looked after by a babysitter a lot of the time. I guess he was hoping that one of the teachers would call home and tell them there was a problem, without necessarily getting him checked out by the nurse first."

"Because he knew that she'd see through him straight off," muttered Hannah. "But Henry must have known that people assumed he was being beaten up by Bruce."

Sam shrugged. "Maybe he didn't care. It wasn't exactly his fault, after all. He never accused him. Anyway, this will be all over the school by Monday morning, so Bruce won't be under suspicion anymore. He glanced at his watch. "We'd better get back. What time d'you want to meet at the fair tomorrow?"

"Don't care. How about eleven?"

"Okay. See you by the main tent." He swallowed the last of his drink, got up, and went off hurriedly, leaving Hannah to make her own way, more slowly, back to Cowleigh Lodge.

*

Every night for the past three weeks, Hannah had drawn another line through the date on the calendar. It looked very different now from the blank page that had fluttered to the ground then, free at last from its long imprisonment. Now, after crossing off June 22, she opened the window wide, got into bed, and lay down. The heat in her bedroom was, if anything, even more oppressive than last night; the air heavier.

Sam had been right—for some reason she didn't feel quite so triumphant about her discovery as she'd have expected. Was it just the lack of sleep and hot, sticky atmosphere . . . or was it a nagging memory of something the bishop had said?

"Just supposing that you were somehow able to obtain proof that this aunt deliberately set out to kill her little niece. How would you feel about that?"

At the time, his words had puzzled her. Now she began to understand why he had asked that particular question.

Because however cleverly she might have traced the crime, just at that moment she couldn't shake off the feeling that it was simply a nasty little story that would have been better left buried. . . .

But within minutes, she was asleep and dreaming, not of Maisie, but of Henry Knight. He was being chased around the school playground by a witch. Only it wasn't a witch; it was Mrs. Jennings, the school nurse, and she had a big stick. "Come here, child!" she was shrieking. "I'm going to beat you until you're black and blue! Black and blue all over!"

twenty-four

THE FAIR

THE MIDSUMMER FAIR WAS held, as it had been for as
long as anyone could remember, on an area of open
ground known as John's Field, about half a mile from
the city center. The fair was as old as the cathedral
itself—some said even older, for though it had been
granted a royal charter in 1215, it had probably been
in existence long before then. At first it had simply
been a market for horses and cattle, an annual event
lasting three days in the third week of June, where bar-
gains were made and scores settled, and fights broke
out as ale flowed freely and tempers ran high. Thieves,
peddlers, and traveling entertainers, attracted by the
edgy, risk-taking mood of the crowd, flocked to the
city in large numbers, knowing that in those three
days, when the daylight lasted well into late evening,

rich pickings were to be had that might keep a family in food over the long, harsh winter.

Little changed for seven hundred years or so. Then, around the middle of the twentieth century, the number of horses and cattle began to dwindle, the peddlers and entertainers increased, and now the ancient tradition had morphed into something more like a huge carnival, with roller coasters, Ferris wheels, bumper cars, and theme rides. But the jugglers, clowns, and acrobats still remained; the music of sedate merry-go-rounds and organ grinders jangled softly but discordantly with the blare of rock music from the loudspeaker system, and people in old-fashioned dress demonstrated weaving and chair mending alongside rifle ranges and carnival games with their displays of cheap jewelry, plastic dolls, and enormous overstuffed teddy bears.

It was all a bit of a mess, thought Hannah, picking her way through the crowds to the main tent, where she'd arranged to meet Sam. But quite a nice mess. As if the city's history, usually perceived as a three-dimensional image stretching back into a distant and indistinct blur, had suddenly been flattened out and allowed to splurge chaotically on the dry, sun-bleached grass of John's Field.

Sam was waiting for her. "You're late," he said. "We've just missed the sky skimmer."

"Oh? Well, we can go on it next time around, can't we?" She had no idea what a sky skimmer might be but didn't much like the sound of it. "How about the helter-skelter?"

"That's for little kids," he said scornfully. "I wouldn't be seen dead on it. Come on, the waltzer's just finished. We'll go on that first."

Hannah spent the next hour and a half with her eyes tight shut, clinging desperately to an iron bar while she hurtled around a succession of rides in a variety of different directions, most of them unexpected and all highly unsettling. Then she sent Sam off to do exactly the same thing all over again for another hour and a half while she let her stomach return to its correct position and observed the crowd. Before leaving home, she had put her sketch pad in the light shoulder bag that held her wallet, and now she took it out.

The fair was always a good opportunity for drawing people, as they were far too engrossed in the noise and spectacle to notice her, so she wandered over to a spot between a merry-go-round, a hoop-throwing game, and a Punch and Judy tent and settled down on the grass. The midday heat was sweltering, though now the sun was hidden behind a thick haze. Hannah wiped her sticky hands on a tissue, took out a pencil, and began to draw.

She drew anxious mothers watching nervous toddlers, anxious toddlers watching nervous mothers, grinning fathers watching laughing children, a gaggle of teenage girls pretending not to watch a group of teenage boys, a bored fairground attendant handing out hoops in threes and watching nobody in particular.

At last she stopped drawing and sat up straight, wiping the sweat from her forehead and stretching her limbs, which were stiff from being so long in one position.

"Can I see?" asked a voice from behind her.

Startled, she turned around. "Oh! Hi, Emily. How long have you been there?"

Emily chuckled. "About ten minutes. You were so busy, you didn't even hear me say hello." She bent down and took the sketchbook from Hannah's hands, slowly turning the pages. "Mmm. Nice," she said appreciatively. "Very nice, in fact. It's weird, isn't it?"

"What is?"

"These faces. Mothers, fathers, young kids, older kids. People must have watched each other just like that for centuries, at this fair. The rides and the stalls may have changed, but the people haven't, have they? I bet if you'd been here, say, six hundred years ago, the expressions you'd have drawn wouldn't have been so very different."

Hannah shrugged. "I guess people are still the same. Relationships can't have changed much, even if everything else has."

"No. Obviously." Emily shook her head. "I don't know why it just struck me then. It must have something to do with this place, at this time of year. You feel kind of . . . *connected*. Know what I mean?"

Hannah looked at her curiously. It was unlike the practical, efficient Emily to let her imagination get the better of her. "Actually, I do know what you mean." She smiled and stood up. "I'm going to find Sam. D'you want to join us? We'll probably do the games and stuff this afternoon."

"No thanks," Emily said quickly. "You'll have a better time on your own. Anyway, I haven't got enough cash for that kind of thing. There are going to be displays and things later on, though. Maybe see you then."

Hannah watched her walk away and was about to set off in search of Sam when his mother approached, a twin holding either hand.

"If you're looking for Sam, he's over there." Eve jerked her head in the general direction of the fast rides. "Hurtling around like a lunatic on those bumper cars. I'm just trying to keep these two out of trouble till their big moment."

Jack and Jessie were looking perfectly docile, as usual, though oddly dressed. Jack had long shorts, jaggedly cut off below the knee, with a little green vest and a hat with a feather in it, and Jessie was wearing a lacy white blouse beneath a flowered pinafore, a couple of sizes too large and roughly tacked up at the hem.

"Costume parade," explained Eve.

"Ah! Hansel and Gretel?" hazarded Hannah.

"Peter Pan and Wendy."

"Of course. Sorry. What time is the parade?"

"Six thirty in front of the main tent. Do me a favor and make sure Sam's there, will you? I don't want him flying around on some infernal machine when he's supposed to be watching his brother and sister."

"If necessary I'll drag him there by his ankles," promised Hannah.

"Good girl. See you later." Eve marched off with the twins trotting by her side like a pair of obedient little dogs. "Good luck!" Hannah called after them.

When she reached the bumper cars, Sam was just climbing out of a car and searching his pocket for change, so Hannah hauled him off before he had a chance to pay for another ride. "Lunchtime," she said firmly.

They bought hamburgers, fries, and two cans

of Coke from a nearby stand and ate standing up, chatting with a little group of friends from school. Afterward, Sam and Hannah wandered among the amusement stands, proceeding to spend a lot of time, and a surprising amount of cash, lobbing coconuts, throwing hoops, attempting to get Ping-Pong balls into goldfish bowls, and testing their strength with a mallet. Three hours later, Sam was the proud owner of a china dog, a pencil case shaped like a fish, and a giant inflatable rabbit. Hannah had only one trophy, an ugly glass vase, and that only because she'd accidentally collared it with a hoop while aiming at a little green jug next to it.

"What are we going to do with all this junk?" Sam looked irritably at his armful of prizes as though it had landed on him uninvited.

Hannah giggled. He looked like one of Santa's elves unable to locate the right chimney. "We could go and find somewhere to sit down, maybe." She glanced at her watch and gave a guilty start. "Hey! I just remembered I told your mom we'd be at the costume parade. We'd better go and get a seat on the grass."

Sam groaned. "Do we have to? It'll be the same boring old thing we've seen every year. Anyway, Jack and Jessie won't know if we're there or not, with all those other kids around."

"That's not the point. Your mother'll know, and I promised her." Hannah led the way firmly through the crowded field toward the big striped tent where people went to report lost property and missing children. Just behind it was a bandstand, where men were seated in tight uniforms, mopping their brows and getting instruments into position.

Sam and Hannah piled their winnings in a heap and slumped down on the tired, flattened grass.

"Aha! I thought I recognized two familiar faces!"

A small, neat figure was approaching, carrying a plaid rug and a wicker basket that seemed to have sprouted leaves.

"Oh. Hello, Miss Murdoch." Hannah smiled at her. "Would you like to join us?" She moved away from Sam, patting the ground between them, and Millie gratefully spread out her rug. "Well, if you don't mind . . ." She put the basket on the rug and sat down next to it. "I have just been buying one or two medicinal plants from a stand over there. They are particularly effective when gathered just now. In fact, there used to be a tradition of throwing certain herbs onto the great bonfires that used to be lit on Midsummer's Eve, as a protection against evil spirits. Afterward, the young men would take turns leaping over the flames. It was said that he who leaped highest would determine the height of the harvest that year!" Miss Murdoch's eyes lit up at the thought of what sounded to Hannah like a thoroughly dangerous game.

"Didn't people sometimes, um, misjudge it?"

"What? Oh, quite possibly, I should think." Millie looked quite unconcerned. "Such a magical time of year, don't you think?" she continued, eyes still shining. "The great solstice! One can almost *feel* the earth holding its breath, pausing on its axis—just for a moment—as it waits for the sun to begin its slow decline into the dark night of winter!"

Hannah smiled politely and Sam stared, but Miss Murdoch continued undaunted, her tone dramatically lowered. "The longest night of the year—when we wake from our dreams to see the world through new eyes. Ah! Shakespeare knew a thing or two about Midsummer!"

"Though I believe the action of the play takes place in May, not June," observed a mild voice from behind. All three of them turned to see the bishop, who had arrived unnoticed with his wife and a couple of folding garden chairs, which he began to set up on the grass.

Miss Murdoch looked slightly put out at being corrected on a technical point, but she knew a bishop when she saw one and gave him a rather frosty smile.

"And of course," he went on, easing his large frame onto the flimsy wooden one, "today is also the Eve of the Feast of St. John the Baptist, for whom this field is named."

"John's Field?" said Hannah, surprised. "I never knew that."

"I did!" said a voice nearby.

"You would," muttered Sam, instantly recognizing Emily's bright, confident tones.

Hannah dug him sharply in the ribs. "Hi, Emily, you found us! Come and sit down."

"Thanks." Emily settled herself on the ground next to the bishop's wife.

"And do you know how the field got its name?" The bishop smiled encouragingly, unaware that when it came to the imparting of historical information, or in fact any information at all, Emily never needed to be asked twice.

"Of course. There's a legend that once there was a holy well in this field, dedicated to St. John the Baptist. The Baptist's Well, it was called. People came here at Midsummer to drink the water and be healed, because it was at this time of the year that the power was said to be at its strongest."

"Quite right, my dear." The bishop nodded approvingly. "Though unfortunately, there is no trace of a well here now. The legend dates from the Middle Ages, when the land around here was much wilder than it is now. This field is thought to be all that is left of a much larger wooded area that gradually disappeared as the city expanded to the west. If there was ever a holy well here, I daresay it is buried now under a great deal of concrete." He smiled sadly.

"But the magic will still be there," said Miss Murdoch, unwilling to let the bishop have it all his own way. "You can't destroy a powerful force like that!"

"Magic?" He cocked an eyebrow. "I thought it was miracles that we were discussing."

"Ah! What's in a name? The thing is that those healing properties were discovered long before any saint came along to claim them. The force is strongest at this time of year because the earth must obey the commands of its master, the sun. The pagans were here first, bishop. You can't deny that!"

"I'm not denying anything," protested the bishop, wiping his brow with a large white handkerchief. "It's far too hot." He turned to Sam and lowered his voice. "I noticed you on those bumper things earlier. Couldn't help thinking it looked like a lot of fun."

"Fantastic," agreed Sam. "You should try it sometime."

"Really? D'you think so? But . . . aren't those cars

rather small for someone like me?"

"They're built for two. You could take one on your own."

"I hadn't thought of that." The bishop's face brightened. "It would have to be at a time when there weren't many people about, of course, like at the end of the day, perhaps, or—"

"Don't be ridiculous, Michael," said his wife, overhearing the conversation and rolling her eyes good-humoredly. "Whatever would people think if they saw you hurtling around a fairground attraction like some teenage hooligan? It would be all around the diocese in no time. And just imagine if the local paper got a picture!"

"I suppose you're right." He sighed regretfully as the band struck up a military march.

"Of course I'm right." She patted his knee. "Now pay attention. The parade's about to start."

While they had been talking, the children had assembled themselves into a long, straggly line, and now they began to slowly file past the panel of judges. There were princes and princesses, knights in armor, Cinderellas with brooms, witches with cauldrons, wizards with tall pointed hats, fairies with flashing wands and tinsel wings. The twins were shuffling along beside a boy dressed in green with an enormous potted plant (presumably Jack and his beanstalk) and another boy on stilts (presumably the giant), wielding a rubber ax. There was even a dragon, played by two children in a lumpy blue suit with red spots, which was having difficulty keeping its sense of direction and had to be shepherded back by a helpful member of the crowd when it strayed out of line. Traditionally, the parade had had a fairy-tale theme, but over the years this had come to be loosely interpreted, and there were also Batmen, Supermen, Spider-Men (and -Women), vampires and vampire slayers, a couple of werewolves, and several Harry Potter look-alikes with jagged scars painted on their foreheads.

The bishop, having apparently recovered from his disappointment at not being allowed on the bumper cars, joined in vociferously with the crowd as it cheered the heroes and booed the villains.

Hannah smiled and stretched out on the grass. In spite of the noise going on around her (Sam, Emily, and even Miss Murdoch were heckling cheerfully), she felt curiously detached—even drowsy. It was such a pleasant, timeless scene, one that must have been enacted in this field year after year, with different children, different costumes, but all with the same theme—the great struggle between good and evil. Victim and predator, innocent and knowing, captive and deliverer. Had the world always been so simple? Was it still?

The glare from the sun had entirely vanished now, and a light wind had sprung up. Hannah closed her eyes, thinking of Millie's impassioned little speech. Did the earth really pause, the way she said, as it sensed the approach of the solstice? And if so, would it be possible to know when the exact moment arrived?

Then she heard it. At first the sound was faint, seeming to come from some way off. But as she listened it intensified, separating itself from the noise of the crowd like a distant siren: not loud so much as urgent. Insistent. It was the sound of a weeping child.

She sat up, shading her eyes with her hand in an effort to see where the child was. And then her heart seemed to stand still, because there, less than fifty yards away, was a little girl. A slender little girl with long dark hair, loose on her shoulders, wearing a knee-length white dress with a deep-frilled hem and a light-blue sash.

twenty-five

MIDSUMMER NIGHTMARE

Hannah blinked, praying that when she opened
her eyes again, the little girl would have disappeared
or been gathered up by a comforting parent and led
back into the parade. But no one came to claim her.
No one even appeared to notice that she was there,
though she was still crying quite audibly.

Hannah tried to get Sam's attention, but he didn't
respond to her shaking his arm, or to her frantic
pointing, and it was clear from the smiling faces of the
bishop, his wife, Emily, and Miss Murdoch that none
of them had the faintest idea what was going on.

She covered her ears with her hands and made
herself look away, still desperately hoping that if
she pretended not to have noticed, the vision might
simply evaporate. But when she turned back, the

child was still there.

It was no good. There was no ignoring the miserable certainty that if she didn't help that little girl, no one else was going to.

Taking a deep breath, she stood up and began to move quickly through the seated spectators. She clambered over feet, dogs, and the remains of picnics, dodging crawling babies and toddling toddlers, occasionally tripping over blankets and buggies, but nobody seemed to mind. In fact, nobody seemed to notice her. At last she reached the narrow strip of roped-off ground between the edge of the crowd and the stalls of the fair; from there it was a clear run to the spot where she had last seen Maisie. Or possibly— she still clung to a faint hope—not Maisie.

Except that she wasn't there now. Minutes ago, Hannah had more than anything wanted the child to disappear. Now her only terror was that it seemed her wish had been granted. Had she sent Maisie away, back to some dark place where she might remain weeping forever? Feverishly she scanned the line of children, still shuffling slowly along. There were several little girls dressed as fairies and princesses—even a couple of Alice in Wonderlands similarly dressed—but none of them was a child who looked quite like Maisie Holt.

Then her eye caught a flash of something white.

It was some way off, near the arcade games, and when she looked again it had vanished. But it had been Maisie, Hannah was certain.

Hannah began to run. Past the plant stall, the hot-dog stand, around the back of the Punch and Judy tent, through a little group of people watching an acrobatic display, until she reached the brightly lit, flashing arcade. But here there were only three or four teenage boys, and a couple of older men wordlessly pushing coins into slots. There was no sign of a little girl in a white dress.

Hannah turned away and peered in each direction. She blinked. Was that Maisie? Over there by the waltzer? Threading her way through the maddeningly slow-moving crowd, she got within twenty yards of the raised platform and scanned the figures standing by the edge. But if it had been Maisie she had seen earlier, she wasn't there now.

And then Hannah spotted her. All the way over on the other side of the field, high up on the sky skimmer, sat a little girl in white, her long dark hair streaming in the wind. Without pausing to wonder how she could have gotten there so quickly, Hannah sped off, dodging clowns and jugglers, skirting around the fire eater, almost colliding with a motionless, white-faced mime, but never once daring to take her eyes off the small figure as it circled high above the field.

By the time she reached the sky skimmer, it was already slowing down, and a long line of people stood waiting for the next ride. Ignoring good manners, Hannah pushed her way to the front and watched impatiently as the ride at last came to a standstill and the people began to get off. Eagerly she scrutinized each figure as it descended. There were giggling girls, swaggering boys, whimpering children, and dazed-looking parents, but not one of them was Maisie Holt.

In desperation, Hannah tugged at the sleeve of the man taking money. "Did you see that little girl? The one in the white dress? She was up there just now! You must have seen her get on. Where did she go?"

But the man didn't reply and went on taking money as if he hadn't heard her.

Then her eye fell on a group of three life-size, face-less cutout figures, about fifty yards away. One was a policeman with a truncheon, another a cowboy brandishing a gun; the third was a ballet dancer in a tutu, standing en pointe. Behind each figure stood a real person whose grinning face filled the empty hole, while parents and friends took photos. But it wasn't the faces that Hannah was staring at. Just for a second, from behind the policeman, she had spied a wisp of long dark hair, and beneath, the edge of a white dress.

She tried to run forward, but the crowd was thicker now, and wherever she moved, someone blocked her way. By dodging and peering, she managed to keep sight of the crudely painted caricatures, until, when she was still twenty yards away, a figure stepped out from behind the policeman. For a second, Hannah stood quite still, not daring to move. And then a wave of disappointment broke over her, for it wasn't Maisie at all but a middle-aged woman with dyed black hair, wearing a skimpy white sundress.

Hannah was moving again now, not because there was anywhere to go, but because the crowd, relentlessly pressing in on her from all sides, carried her with it. From time to time she thought she could see a glimpse of a white dress, a head of dark hair like Maisie's, but without a hope of being able to reach it. She started to panic. Why were there so many people suddenly? And why did they jostle and push her like this? Dimly, she knew that she should get back to the costume parade, because Sam and the bishop and Miss Murdoch would be wondering where she'd gone. But for some reason, she'd lost her sense of direction and couldn't remember where the parade was being held, and even if she could, there was no way of getting there unless the ever-growing throng of people chose to go there too.

Suddenly she became aware that the crowd had

stopped moving. It had apparently reached an obstruction. But it wasn't until people began slowly shuffling to the left or right, with Hannah being helplessly drawn to the left, that she realized what the obstruction was, and by that time, she was standing right in front of it.

It was the merry-go-round. A ride must have just finished, because children were scrambling off and new ones getting on. Very soon, nearly all the horses were taken, and the man was going around taking money from outstretched hands. He was about half-way when Hannah saw Maisie.

She was sitting no more than ten yards off, astride a little cream-colored horse with a red-and-gold harness. She was facing away, but there was no mistaking the white dress with its frilled hem and blue sash. And even if there had been a fragment of doubt in Hannah's mind, it would have vanished when she saw that the man taking money passed right by Maisie, just as though the horse had no rider.

This time she wasn't taking any chances. Eagerly, she jumped onto the platform and began threading her way through the ranks of painted horses, her eyes fixed resolutely on the girl in the white dress. But she hadn't gone more than a couple of yards when the wooden slats beneath gave a sudden jerk, music started, and the ride began. Although the platform wasn't moving particularly fast, it was surprisingly difficult to stay upright. She stumbled and would have fallen if the nearest horse, which luckily had no rider, hadn't been there to steady her. Keeping one hand on its back, she edged to the front of the platform, preparing to jump off, but by the time she got there, the ride had picked up just enough speed to make it unsafe. There was nothing to do but mount the horse and sit it out.

As soon as she was in the saddle, she looked anxiously to make sure that Maisie hadn't escaped, but the girl was still there, her dark hair fluttering in the wind. Having made sure of this, Hannah relaxed slightly and began to enjoy the quiet, leisurely pace.

And then, after a moment or two, she began to be anxious again. Little by little, the ride was getting faster. That was odd, because merry-go-rounds weren't like the other rides—they were sedate affairs, usually—yet she could hear no protests from the other children, who all seemed to be sitting quite still on their small mounts. She peered around to see if the watching parents showed signs of concern, and that was when she noticed that the platform suddenly seemed higher than she remembered it. Alarmed, she turned back and saw that Maisie's hair no longer fluttered gently but streamed out behind her.

The ride had now gathered enough speed to

prevent her from seeing the fairground clearly, and as the horses went faster, so did the music. She began to feel giddy, disoriented. Soon the tents and stalls started to merge together. Before long they were a single, seamless belt of color, and still the pace increased relentlessly. The music was getting louder as well as faster. Too loud, surely? She wanted to stick her fingers in her ears, but she didn't dare let go of the horse's neck, so she clung on tightly and tried not to look down at the ground, which seemed to be getting farther away by the minute.

Now Hannah needed all her strength just to stay on. She could no longer sit upright but lay flat against the horse's back, her arms tight around its neck while the jangling, discordant music filled her ears until she thought her head must burst.

It was from this position that she noticed the child directly in front of her.

The sight chilled her. Not a hair on his head was moving. He sat perfectly still, as if he were made of the same wood as the horse beneath.

Staring in terror, she saw that the other children were all equally motionless, their hair and clothes quite undisturbed by the wind that rushed past, and when she forced her gaze out to the watching crowd, she could see that the people there were no more real than the children but simply cutout figures with grinning faces, and all the time the horses hurtled around, faster and faster, and the fairground was no longer a fairground but a confused, dizzying blur, and just as she thought she could bear it no longer, there was a terrible jolting and grinding, and the ride came to an abrupt halt.

Hannah buried her face in the horse's neck. Gradually she became aware that someone was shaking her. "Wake up!" said a voice. "Wake up! Ride's over! Time to get off!"

twenty-six

GATHERING STORM CLOUDS

"WAKE UP! HANNAH! WAKE up, for goodness' sake! What's the matter with you?" She opened her eyes to find Sam bending over her, shaking her shoulder.

She stared up at him, then down at the ground, which was where she was lying.

"Did I . . . fall off?"

"Fall off what?"

"The horse."

"Horse?" He looked startled. "What are you talking about? There's no horse here."

"Yes, there is! I was on it, on the merry-go-round, and Maisie was there too, I was just behind her, but she was going too fast! I couldn't catch her, and . . . and now I've lost her and I'll never be able to find her again in all this—" She stopped. Sam was grinning at her.

"Don't be dumb! You haven't been anywhere. You were asleep right here, all the time the parade was going on. You must have been dreaming."

She sat up stiffly and peered around her. There was the field with the striped tent directly in front, and the bandstand behind, just as it had been—how long ago? Then she noticed that that there was no sign of the costume parade, and Miss Murdoch, the bishop and his wife, and Emily had gone. In fact, there were very few people about, and those who were left were running.

Sam had grabbed hold of her hand and was pulling her up. "Come on. We need to get moving. Fast."

"Where are we going?" She swayed, trying to regain a sense of balance. Not just physical balance— her brain was still struggling to reconcile the opposing forces of fantasy and reality, which for the moment seemed to be having a pitched battle inside her head.

"Back to your place. It's closer than mine. Look at the sky."

She looked up and suddenly realized why everyone was running. The afternoon's haze had disappeared. In its place were sullen black clouds that, as she watched, seemed to draw themselves together, shoulder to shoulder, in preparation for their assault upon the evening. A flash of lightning lit the sky, followed a few seconds later by an ominous rumble, then a deafening crack.

"Don't just stand there, come *on!*" urged Sam as the first fat, heavy drops started to fall.

She shivered and began to run.

Within minutes the rain was falling in torrents, turning litter to pulp and the field to a sea of mud, slowing their progress as they dodged ruts and puddles with plastic ice-cream cups floating like little boats. By the time they were back on the street, shopkeepers were struggling to wind up awnings, and café staff were hurriedly dragging chairs and tables off the sidewalk. Small groups huddled together in doorways, while from behind shop windows steamy with condensation peered faces vague and distorted in the murky light. Those still out and about moved quickly, furtively, flinching every so often as a new flash was followed by another calamitous crack. Umbrellas poked forward over bent heads, like grim shields in some watery battle.

To Hannah, stumbling along blindly, the scene had a nightmarish unreality, as though she hadn't properly woken from one dream before being plunged into the next.

When they reached Cowleigh Lodge, the front door was locked. "D'you have a key?" demanded Sam.

She fumbled in her bag and found the key but for some reason had difficulty fitting it into the lock.

"Give it to me," he muttered, snatching it impatiently and giving it a quick turn.

The door swung open, and they stepped inside.

twenty-seven

SAM

THE MOMENT SAM CLOSED the door behind them, the sounds of the storm stopped. The air smelled damp and the house felt unexpectedly chilly.

He removed his dripping jacket and hung it over the banister post before turning to Hannah, who hadn't moved.

"Hey! What are you waiting for? Aren't you going to take your wet stuff off?"

She slowly slid her arms out of her jacket and stood as if unsure what to do with it. He grabbed it and slung it on top of his own. Then he noticed a note lying on the table next to the telephone. "Looks like your mom had to go out suddenly," he said, glancing at the hastily scrawled script. "You'd better read what she says."

Hannah moved toward the table and stood there, looking down at the message. "I don't understand," she said after a few moments. "Can you explain it, please?"

"Huh?" He looked more closely.

Hannah,

Uncle David's been taken ill. He's in the hospital, so I'm driving up to Birmingham right away. Didn't have time to cook anything, I'm afraid, but there's bread and cheese in the fridge, and I've put out a can of soup. I should be back around eight thirty.

Mom. X

"What's there to understand? Your uncle's sick and she's gone to see him."

"I don't know Uncle David."

"Some kind of distant relative, then? Oh, well." Sam moved away from the telephone table and walked into the living room. The smell of damp was stronger in here; the windows were shut and the curtains drawn. It couldn't be much after eight, but the room was already dark. He stared at the walls, puzzled. Surely, when he'd been here last, they'd looked lighter, paler than this? Going closer to examine them, he saw that the cream paintwork was looking patchy, as if the wall had been given a quick undercoat before being properly covered up. Beneath the uneven streaks were signs of a different color. A kind of dark brown. Yet he could have sworn that the paintwork had looked pretty solid before. "I thought you said it was just upstairs that this house was looking shabby?"

When Hannah didn't reply, he turned around to see her sitting up straight on the sofa, feet together, her hands neatly folded in her lap.

"Are you okay?"

"Okay?"

"Are you all right? You seem a bit quiet."

She didn't reply.

"Oh, well, I guess it's that dream still bothering you, is it? Let's switch the TV on. That'll cheer you up." But when he aimed the remote control at the screen, nothing happened. He got up and pressed the button on top of the set. Still nothing. And when he clicked the light switch by the door, the room remained in shadowy gloom.

"The storm must have brought a power line down," he muttered. "D'you have any candles?"

"There are candles in the kitchen."

He went out to the kitchen and started rummaging in drawers and cupboards. After a minute or so he found candles, a box of matches, and half a dozen saucers. Straightening up, he paused for a moment, looking at the wall units. Between the top of the cupboards and the ceiling was a thin line of discoloration, extending a little beyond the units and continuing downward on either side until it met the counter. It looked like the outline of some large piece of furniture—a cabinet, maybe—that had once stood there. This was an old house, after all. But it was odd that that mark hadn't been painted over when the new kitchen was put in.

He went back into the living room and got busy with the candles, applying a match to the base of each one so that the wax melted just enough to make it stick to the saucer. Hannah didn't offer to help. When he'd finished, he lit the wicks and placed the saucers at strategic spots around the room.

"What shall I do with this?" he asked her when there was only one left without a home.

"Put it on the cabinet."

"What cabinet? Oh!" He chuckled, seeing what she was pointing at. "The TV, you mean." He did what she suggested, then returned to the sofa and surveyed the room. The gentle, flickering light softened outlines and blurred detail, favoring some things but bathing others in deep shadow, creating an oddly ambiguous effect. He had to remind himself that what looked like a small chest of drawers was really Hannah's father's music system, that the shelf of books above contained not books but tapes and CDs, and that the dim, box-like thing crouched on the desk in the corner was actually a computer.

He cast his eye over the shelves and eventually spotted a pile of board games. "Tell you what. How about we play Scrabble? Just till the power comes back on."

He took the box off the shelf, opened the board, and put it on the table in front of the sofa. Then he sat down beside Hannah, placed a letter tray in front of her and another for himself, and offered her the box. She looked at it.

"Go on then, take one."

She picked out a tile. Then he took one. "I've got C. How about you?" He peered at her hand. "P. I'll start." He took another six letters from the box and put them in the tray.

Hannah watched him for a moment or two, then did the same.

"Wait a minute, we need something to score with." He got up to look for paper and a pencil, spied Hannah's schoolbag by the door, and after a few seconds' search in the dim light gave up and tipped the contents onto the floor. He picked up a pencil, unceremoniously tore a blank page from a notebook, and returned to the table. Then he frowned thoughtfully and laid out the word HEART vertically down the center of the board.

"Sixteen," he said, taking five more tiles before writing their names at the top of the torn-off page and the figure below his own. "Your turn."

Hannah picked up two tiles and laid them on either side of the first letter of Sam's HEART. Then she took two more from the box.

"Is that the best you can do? THE?" He looked at her in surprise. "Oh, well." He wrote the number six under her name, then placed four of his own letters downward at the top of the board, above the first letter of her word, spelling GIANT. "Only seven, but it gives you a shot at the triple word score," he said generously.

But Hannah didn't take advantage of his offer. Instead, she used the R from HEART to spell ANSWER.

"Not bad," he conceded. "Only ten points, though. Pity." Taking four replacement tiles from the box, he paused for a moment, listening. For a moment he could have sworn there was someone upstairs. But there couldn't be, of course.

Using the last letter of HEART, he added six more tiles to form TRELLIS. "Nine. Not exactly great scores so far!" He chuckled, but she didn't return his smile, only placing I and N horizontally above the S of TRELLIS.

"Eight. Bit of a waste of that triple word score," he remarked. "Are you still bothered by that dream, or have you just got a lousy bunch of letters?" Without waiting for a reply, he put down BRACE using the first letter of ANSWER and wrote thirteen under his own name.

Hannah added two more letters in front of the E of BRACE.

"Hmm. Another THE. Fourteen points, though. Good work getting the H on that triple letter score," he said encouragingly. Then his eyes lit up as he spied a golden opportunity. Grinning, he spelled TRIFLE using the first letter of Hannah's word, finishing on a triple word score. "Thirty!"

Then he stopped grinning and frowned. He tilted his head toward the ceiling. "Did you leave a radio on in one of the bedrooms?"

She looked at him blankly.

"Because it sounds like there are voices coming from upstairs."

"That will be Ellen and Jane."

"Ellen and Jane? Are they the kids from next door?" He shook his head, puzzled. The noise didn't sound as though it was coming from outside, but presumably it must be. He shrugged and took five more tiles from the box. "Just my luck, nearly all vowels," he muttered.

Hannah laid five letters across the board next to the F of TRIFLE to spell FLYING.

Sam shifted each one a little way off its square to check the score. "Great! Twenty-six." He wrote the figure under Hannah's name, then viewed his own tiles with gloom. After some time, he sighed and placed two letters under the N of FLYING to make NIB. "Five. That's the best I can do."

Hannah added three tiles to the last letter of NIB to spell BIRD, taking advantage of a triple word score beneath the last letter.

"Twenty-one," said Sam. "Not bad for a four-letter word!" He gave her a sly smile, but as before, she didn't respond. He pushed the board away, regarding her thoughtfully. "What's the matter? You've hardly said a word all evening. Are you mad at me or something?"

"Mad?" She looked puzzled. "I hope I am not mad."

Something about the way she said the word made him feel uncomfortable. It sounded wrong. Only he couldn't quite explain why. After a few moments he got up.

"Know what I think? We need to eat something."

He was halfway across the room when her next words stopped him.

"Cook will have left us a cold supper, I daresay."

He turned around and stared. "What did you say?"

"It is her day off, but she always prepares something before she goes out."

"What are you talking about? Have you gone crazy? You don't have a cook!"

She looked shocked. "Has she given notice? Why was I not told of it?"

"Listen," he said, trying to control the edge of fear that had crept into his voice. "If this is some kind of joke, just cut it out! I'm not in the mood. Okay? Now I'm going into the kitchen to fix us something to eat, and when I get back, I'd like to hear a bit of sense for a change!"

He left the room and began opening and closing doors in the kitchen, deliberately making a lot of noise to drown out the alarm bells in his head that were growing louder by the minute. But when he turned around, he saw that she had followed him. She was standing in the doorway, watching him.

"If you want to make yourself useful, you can spread butter on some bread," he said curtly. He opened a can of soup and poured it into two bowls, in his agitation putting them in the microwave and closing the door before remembering that it wouldn't work.

"Why do you put food in a cage? It cannot escape, you know."

"Shut up," he muttered.

"The butter and milk should not be kept in a cupboard in this hot weather. Why are they not in the larder? They will turn rancid."

"Just stop it, will you?" He turned and faced her, red faced and shaking.

A horrible thought occurred to him. She was right. Without electricity, this house had reverted to its original state. The refrigerator was just a cupboard, the microwave a cage; the stove, washing machine, vacuum cleaner, and all the rest of the carefully designed appliances were no more than useless lumber. A waste of space. He pushed past her and ran back into the living room.

The candles were low now, their feeble flames guttering, throwing nervous shadows around the darkened room. And then his blood seemed to run cold. Because now, where the TV had stood, there was a real cabinet, with a lacy cloth covering it, a potted plant sprouting fleshy leaves above. What had been the music system was a small chest of drawers. The shelf had real books, not tapes or CDs, and the computer had become a snakeskin-covered writing case, lying on an elegant polished desk.

An icy sweat broke out on his forehead; he felt dizzy and sick. Blindly he stumbled toward the stairs, the need to get to the bathroom overcoming even his fear of what might lie above. He reached the landing and turned the handle of the bathroom door. It was locked.

"Who's in there?" he shouted.

There was no answer.

"Come out, for god's sake!"

But no sound came from the other side of the door.

Trembling violently, he knelt down and pressed his eye to the keyhole. The room beyond was dimly lit, but he could just make out the shape of a narrow bed, a chair, a small cupboard with a candle burning in a plain white holder. There was no bath, no basin. And where there had once been tiles was now pale, striped wallpaper. Of an occupant there was no sign. The room was empty.

Fear turned the sweat on his forehead clammy; it even stopped the nausea in his throat. He slumped down with his back to the door, and for a few seconds, everything went black.

At last he got to his feet and walked slowly down the stairs.

When he reached the living room, she was waiting

for him. He walked toward her. Then he stopped. He faced her, forcing her to look into his eyes.

"Who am I?"

She held out her hand and smiled politely. "Forgive me. I do not believe we have been introduced. My name is Maisie Holt."

twenty-eight

THE WRONG ROOM

He wanted to run. Out of the room, out of this terrible house, across the city to his own home, with his mother and father and the twins and the noise of the TV and the comforting sounds of the neighbors chatting and shouting and quarreling in the street below.

But he couldn't. Because the girl in front of him, with the blank eyes, the set smile, was his friend. She wasn't Maisie Holt. She was Hannah Price. And if he didn't help her now, no one else was going to.

"Listen, Maisie," he said, trying to keep his voice steady. "We need to leave this house. I'm going to take you away from here." He held out his hand, but she stepped back, frowning.

"Why should I go with you? I do not know who

you are. Besides, if I am not here when Mama returns, how will she know where to find me?"

Although her words chilled him, they also reminded him of something. Hannah's mother. Hadn't she said she would be back by eight thirty? He glanced at the grandfather clock against the wall. Its familiarity was oddly reassuring, for this was one of the few objects in the room he recognized. Only its hands stood at nine fifteen. Where was Mrs. Price?

He tried to think clearly. If Hannah's mother was delayed for some reason, she couldn't call the landline because it wasn't working. Was it possible that she had tried Hannah's cell phone and they hadn't heard it? He had to find it. Still keeping his eyes on Hannah, he backed out of the room. In the hall, he searched feverishly for the bag she'd been wearing on her shoulder that afternoon. At last he found it—or what looked like it in the murky light—lying on the floor where she must have dropped it when they'd first come in. He groped inside until his hand met something cold and hard and oblong.

Withdrawing it, he felt eagerly for the keypad. Then suddenly his fingers lost their grip and the object fell to the floor with a light clatter. For the thing he'd been holding wasn't a cell phone. It was like something he'd seen once before, on a visit to the city museum—a Victorian metal spectacle case.

He leaned heavily against the banister rail, his knees trembling. The house was very still. The only sound came from the grandfather clock, quietly measuring out the seconds.

The open door to the living room showed only a single candle burning now, low and erratic. But he didn't want to go in there. Slowly he groped his way toward the kitchen. Then, in the doorway, he stopped, rigid with shock.

The dwindling light was just enough to define the outline of a room he no longer recognized. Where the refrigerator had stood was now a tall, brown-painted cupboard. There was no gleaming white oven—only a soot-blackened range. The dishwasher, the cabinets, the counter had all vanished, and in their place was a deep square sink with a rough board beside it, a scrubbed wooden table, and a tall cabinet hung with patterned cups.

A few seconds later, the light from across the hall finally died. The last candle had gone out.

It was utterly dark in the room now. And with the darkness came silence, thick and heavy. He strained his ears for sounds from outside but could hear no voices, no hum of distant traffic. A new terror seized him. What if it wasn't only this house that had changed? Supposing they were both trapped in some freak time warp, forced to spend the rest of their lives in an alien century? He tried to look out the window, but he could see nothing beyond the misty glass. If the real world existed out there, the house had shut it out. Sealed itself off. It seemed to hold its breath. Waiting.

A low whining noise almost made him jump out of his skin. Simultaneously, the kitchen leaped into light. The dresser, the range, the brown-painted cupboard, the scrubbed table had all vanished. The cabinets and counter were back, the electric clock was ticking on the wall, the refrigerator was humming, and from the living room came the sound of a man's voice announcing a news item. It was a little while before he realized that in addition to all this, the phone was ringing in the hall.

He stumbled toward it and picked up the receiver. "Hello?"

"Sam? Is that you?" Mrs. Price sounded anxious. "I've been trying to reach Hannah all evening. Do you know where she is?"

A sound from behind made him look around to see a bewildered-looking Hannah standing in the doorway of the living room, rubbing her eyes. "Who's that?" The voice sounded sleepy, but it was hers.

Weak with relief, he turned back to the phone. "She's right here," he breathed. "I'll hand you over."

After giving her the receiver, Sam stayed in the hall for a few moments listening to her talk—not because he needed to know what she said, just for the comfort of hearing her voice. Hannah Price's voice. Then, after switching off the noise from the TV in the living room, he ran quickly up the stairs.

The bathroom door was ajar now, revealing the room's plain white interior. Only a very faint blue stripe where there was a missing tile gave a disturbing reminder of that terrifying glimpse through the keyhole. He crossed the landing and pushed open the door of the empty room. The walls were still damaged, discolored, but no worse than before. Nothing had changed. He glanced in through the door to Hannah's parents' room. Here again, all seemed normal, so far as he could tell.

He was about to check on Hannah's bedroom when a noise from above stopped him. A light, uneven tapping sound. Looking up, he noticed that in a corner of the ceiling just outside her room, there was a bulge underneath the plaster, where water had collected and was dripping onto the floor below. He had forgotten all about the rain, but now he remembered the smell of damp when they'd first come in.

Somewhere there must be a hole in the roof. He went back into the bathroom, found an enamel bowl on a shelf, and placed it on the floor of the landing to catch the drips.

When he got back downstairs, Hannah was putting the phone down. "Uncle David's not well."

"I know. That's what it said in the note."

"What note?"

Sam swallowed. This was going to need careful handling. He decided to play for time. "Is he . . . seriously sick?"

"No, thank goodness. They thought it might be viral pneumonia, but it turns out it's just a bad chest infection. Mom was going to come back after seeing him, but she called to say she'll stay with my aunt tonight because she doesn't like driving in bad weather. She said she didn't mind leaving me here if you could stay. You can stay, can't you?"

"Yes. Listen. Do you . . . um . . . remember anything about what happened this evening?"

"I remember the storm, and getting back here. Then I guess I must have fallen asleep on the sofa. The phone woke me. Why? Was there a problem?"

Since a truthful answer to this was quite likely to give her nightmares for the next ten years, if not for the rest of her life, he didn't reply. The trouble was, if she hadn't been mentally traumatized by what had happened that night, he had. He still couldn't get rid of the sense that, just before the power was restored, the house had been on the point of some revelation. What if that revelation was still to come? Hannah was going to have to find out sooner or later.

She solved the immediate problem by suggesting they have something to eat.

This time it was she who prepared the meal while he stood in the doorway and watched her heating the soup in the microwave and making sandwiches. Glancing around the kitchen, rechecking its contents, Sam's eye fell on the little wooden box.

"Is this where you found the locket?"

She nodded.

He raised the lid, peered inside, and then pulled open the little papier-mâché box. "Ugh! These are teeth? That's gross! Who'd want to keep disgusting things like that?"

"A mother. Mom says she kept some of my first teeth, and"—she gave him a sly glance—"I wouldn't mind betting yours did too."

"You think so?" He shook his head in disbelief. Then he unfolded the handkerchief, with its carefully sewn message:

To Dearest Mama
From your Loving
Daughter Maisie
Aged 9 years and 2 months

He regarded it thoughtfully for a few moments. "Did you say the box was found in your parents' room?"

"Yes. Under the floorboards."

"And they're sleeping in the smaller room at the front? The one with a single window?"

"Yes."

"Why?"

Hannah looked at him, puzzled. "You know why. It's because we can't use the big room. Otherwise they'd have chosen that one. Obviously. It's by far the nicer of the two."

"I don't mean why are they sleeping there. I mean why, when that room's so much better, did you find the box in the *other* one?"

Hannah paused in the act of spreading butter, suddenly realizing the significance of this. Mrs. Holt would presumably have been able to choose any room she liked, so it seemed odd that she'd been prepared to settle for that one, while giving the larger room to her sister-in-law, whom she clearly didn't like much.

Then Hannah shrugged and went back to making the sandwich. "Maybe she didn't like being woken early. The big room probably gets more light in the mornings. Come on. Let's eat."

They had their meal sitting at the kitchen table. Sam said little, seeming preoccupied. Every so often he stole a glance at the box. "Those initials on the lid," he said after a little while. "L.H. Presumably they're Mrs. Holt's?"

"They must be."

"Do you know what her first name was?"

"No . . . I don't think anyone mentioned a first name."

A few minutes later he pushed his plate away, though there was still half a sandwich left. "What did you do with that photograph?"

Hannah screwed up her eyes in an effort to remember. "I think I put it on the telephone table. It's probably gotten covered by a whole lot of other things since, though. Why?"

But Sam was already out of the room. She heard him shifting papers around; then a small grunt of satisfaction told her he'd found the photo. After that came silence.

"Sam?" she called, when half a minute had gone by and he still hadn't returned. "Are you okay?"

Slowly he walked back into the kitchen, carrying the photograph. Only it wasn't the front he was looking at. It was the back. He laid it facedown on the table and pointed to something written there in pencil. It was very faint, which must have been why she hadn't noticed it before, but it was still just legible. It said:

Mrs. Caroline Holt, Miss Laetitia Holt, Maisie Holt, with staff at Cowleigh Lodge. September 1875.

Hannah stared at the names, trying somehow to make the neat, faded lettering fit into the pattern they'd so carefully worked out. But it was no good. There seemed to be only one possible interpretation of the evidence in front of them. And that was that the little box of treasures had belonged not to Maisie's mother, but to her aunt. The woman who had apparently hated her niece so much that she was prepared to kill her.

twenty-nine

CONNECTING

"I JUST DON'T GET it," said Hannah at last. "No one who wanted to keep the stuff in that box could possibly have harmed the child it all belonged to. Mom was right. It's a *mother's* box."

"Well, where does that leave us? Are you suggesting that Laetitia wasn't Maisie's aunt at all, but her *mother?*" He turned the photograph over, and silently they examined the faces of the pretty child, the ugly woman.

"No." Hannah shook her head. "It's impossible. And not only because Maisie's face is nothing like Laetitia's—she's the image of Mrs. Holt. You can see that if she'd lived, she would have been just like her."

"Only she didn't live," said Sam, lightly tracing the outline of the little girl with his finger. "What did Sherlock Holmes say? 'When you have eliminated the impossible, whatever remains, *however improbable*, must be the truth.'"

"Which is?"

"That if Laetitia Holt didn't poison Maisie, then somebody else did." The stark sentence lay between them, flat and uncompromising as the photograph.

"But Inspector Bean said that the hair sample showed prolonged exposure to arsenic poisoning," Hannah muttered. "That means that only someone with very close access to Maisie would have had the chance to do it without being detected."

"Exactly." His voice was grim.

"You mean . . . ?"

He nodded. "I think it has to be one of the people in this photograph."

Again they examined the stern faces, the stiff poses. Sam shook his head. "They all look like murderers!"

"They just look scared. I don't suppose they'd ever been photographed before."

"Scared of a man with a camera? Maybe," he mused. "But if we're right, one of them had enough guts to slowly and deliberately poison a little kid. They must have known the risk they were taking. If anyone had found out, well . . ." He drew a finger swiftly underneath his chin to indicate a grisly death.

"Why, though? There'd have to be a motive. What would any of these people have had to gain from killing Maisie?"

"How about that old lady? Could you talk to her again?"

"And ask her if her grandmother might have been a poisoner? Are you crazy? Anyway, she was only a child herself when she heard about it, and it sounds as if she just swallowed the idea that Miss Holt was responsible, like everyone else seems to have done, including anyone who might have employed her later. According to Mrs. Wilson, she never found work anywhere else job and died soon after in the workhouse."

"So whoever it was did a good job of framing her." Sam's voice was somber.

"And we're not going to find out who, are we? Not now?" Hannah pushed the photograph away and ran her fingers through her hair. "I wish I'd never discovered all that about the arsenic! What good has it done? Just given us a mystery we've no hope of solving!"

Sam didn't reply. He glanced around the kitchen, so innocent now in its bland, modern efficiency. Yet less than an hour ago it had been a living nightmare. Again he had the sense that the house had been trying to tell them something. It was as if the absence of electrical power had stirred a memory within its walls, allowing the candlelight briefly to re-create a moment in time that, with the return of the harsh light, had now dissolved, perhaps never to return.

But he couldn't share any of this with Hannah because, unlike him, she had to go on living here. That was when he remembered the Scrabble board. He hadn't put it away after the game, so it must be still there. Thank goodness he'd thought of it before she saw it first!

"D'you mind if I leave you to clear the supper things away?" he said casually. "I should just call Mom and tell her I'm staying here tonight."

"You don't need to. My mother said she'd let her know."

"Oh? Well, I'll call her anyway, just so she doesn't worry."

Fortunately, Hannah seemed too preoccupied with her own thoughts to notice anything suspicious in Sam's sudden display of consideration for his mother's feelings, or his need for privacy. She simply nodded and began to gather up the plates and bowls.

The Scrabble board was just as they'd left it, the unfinished game with its random selection of words sprawled unevenly across the grid. He was about to pick it up and tip the tiles back into the box when he paused. He hadn't taken much notice at the time, but now it struck him as odd that so many of Hannah's words were short—two or three letters at most. And the word THE appeared twice. Then he noticed something else. Apart from one tiny exception, every single contribution from her had been set down horizontally.

There was a hot, prickling feeling in his forehead—half excitement, half fear—as he carefully removed his own words, leaving only hers. And what he saw was this.

T H E

A N S W E R   I N
                  S

T H E

F L Y I N G

B I R D

"Sam? Are you still on the phone?" Hannah was calling from the kitchen.

"Just saying good night to the twins!" he called

back. "Won't be long." He seized the board, slid the tiles back into the box, folded the square of cardboard over the top, and replaced the lid. Feverishly, his eyes scanned the room. A picture on the wall showed seagulls wheeling over a stormy sea, but they were lightly sketched and indistinct. In any case, there were several of them, not just one, and they all looked much the same. There was a china bird on the mantelpiece, but a quick examination showed nothing unusual. It was simply a china bird. What, then? Had he missed something? Was there still some relic from those minutes when the house had been without electricity—an object from the past, left behind, stranded out of time? But however hard he searched, there was nothing else in that room remotely like a flying bird.

An unpleasant thought struck him. Was it some kind of joke? He'd heard of mischievous spirits who hid possessions for weeks until their owners eventually found them in the place they'd looked a hundred times. Supposing Maisie had just been playing with them? She was only a kid, after all.

After a few moments he put the Scrabble box back on the shelf and walked slowly back to the kitchen.

"I've been thinking," said Hannah, frowning as she put away cutlery in a drawer, "that it's odd we just accepted the fact that whatever bad thing happened

223

to Maisie, her aunt must have been responsible. Why did we never question it?"

"Because, according to that old lady you talked to, the servants never questioned it. Laetitia'd done all the nursing, even tried to get Maisie moved to her own room, so it must have looked like she was trying to get total control over her. Anyway, they all thought she was a witch, didn't they? Let's face it, she looks like one! And didn't you say Maisie had those weird bruises that suddenly appeared overnight?"

Hannah nodded. What had Mrs. Wilson said? That Maisie had been, literally, black and blue. For some reason, the words bothered her. Why? She wandered slowly back and forth, putting things away, wiping down surfaces, only half concentrating on what she was doing.

"Though if we're right, and it was really one of these people trying to frame her—" Sam broke off, as Hannah had suddenly spun around and was agitatedly waving a dishcloth at him. "What's the matter? Why are you looking at me like that?"

"Listen! *Who else do we know with a load of unexplained bruises?*"

"Huh?" He stared at her. "Oh. Henry Knight, you mean? But those weren't real bruises; they were just fake. They were eye makeup, for heaven's sake!"

"And what color is eye makeup?"

"You're asking me?" He looked bewildered. "Well, black, I guess. And blue. Gray, maybe. Dark colors, anyway."

"And what else did we find in the attic, besides the doll?"

He screwed up his eyes, trying to remember. "Oh! That paint box?"

"Exactly! And it was all the *dark* colors that were used up!"

For once Sam was silent, and an image seemed to rise before them, of a long-dead little girl, hiding herself away, secretly mixing her paints with water, artfully dabbing them onto her smooth, white skin.

Then Hannah shook her head. "It doesn't prove anything. For all we know, I was right and Maisie just liked painting gloomy pictures. And if we're also right about the nightmares being hers, then she would have had a good reason for being depressed."

"A good enough reason to deliberately frame her aunt?"

"We don't know that she did."

"No? Henry did, though, didn't he?" said Sam. "He knew perfectly well that Bruce would get the blame for his injuries because he was the obvious suspect. He *looks* like a bully, just like Laetitia *looked* like a witch.

There was no need for either of them to do more than throw out odd hints. Natural prejudice would take care of the rest."

"And in Laetitia's case, that prejudice led to her death in the workhouse," muttered Hannah, shuddering. "But why? What could have made her hate her aunt so much?"

"Maybe she didn't," said Sam.

"Huh?"

"Think about it. Did Henry fake those bruises because he hated Bruce? He hardly knows him."

"Of course. But he had another motive. He was just trying to get his parents' attention," said Hannah.

"Exactly!"

"What? Oh!" Her jaw dropped. "You think Maisie could have been . . . ?"

But Sam was thoughtfully drawing the photograph toward him. "I think it's time we had a look at the *other* person in the picture."

MRS. WILSON

"THIS IS MAISIE'S MOTHER, right?" Sam pointed to the dark-haired woman—one of the seated figures in the little group.

"Yes." Hannah had drawn up a chair next to him, and together they looked closely at the pretty face, so like Maisie's own.

"What do we know about her?"

"Not a lot. Mrs. Wilson hardly mentioned her." Now that she considered this, it seemed odd that such an important figure in Maisie's life had been left out of the picture. In fact, she thought, scrutinizing the slightly abstracted expression, it almost looked as though Mrs. Holt hadn't wanted to be in the picture at all.

"Do you know what happened to her after Maisie died?" asked Sam.

"She left and the house was sold. I suppose it had too many sad memories for her."

"Where did she go?"

"I've no idea. You're not suggesting that Maisie's *mother* had anything to do with what happened to her, are you?" She looked at him in alarm.

"I'm not suggesting anything. I just think it's weird that we know so little about this woman."

Hannah cast her mind back to the conversation with Pat Wilson. There had been something slightly strange about it. A sense that she was holding something back. Something that disturbed her. "You're right," she said slowly. "I've a feeling Mrs. Wilson didn't want to talk about Maisie's mother."

Sam looked at his watch. "It's ten forty-five. Too late to call her now. We'll have to wait till tomorrow morning."

Hannah nodded dejectedly. The she suddenly sat up straight. "No, we won't! She told me her phone's always switched off when she's asleep and I could call her any time I liked."

"Well, then."

"D'you want me to do it? What shall I say?"

"Just ask her what she knows about Mrs. Holt."

Hannah didn't argue with him, but she felt slightly ridiculous calling someone up at this time of night to ask about a woman who'd probably been dead for a century. Nevertheless, she fetched her cell phone, set it on speaker so that Sam could hear the conversation, and pressed the number.

"Pat Wilson." The voice answered almost immediately.

"Hello, Mrs. Wilson. Sorry to call so late. It's Hannah Price here. I came to see you last weekend to ask about Cowleigh Lodge. Do you remember?"

"Of course. What can I do for you, dear? Nothing wrong, is there?"

"Not exactly. I just wondered if you or Mrs. Grocott could tell us anything about Maisie's mother.'

"What did you what to know?"

Was it Hannah's imagination, or had the tone changed, very slightly? "Um, anything, really. What kind of a person was she?"

"She was a beautiful woman. But you can see that from the photo, can't you?"

"Yes. Of course. Only she looks a bit, well, *distant*, really. Were she and Maisie close, do you know?"

"Close? They were mother and daughter, weren't they?"

Hannah looked helplessly at Sam. This wasn't getting them anywhere!

"Ask her how she coped with Maisie's illness!" he

whispered urgently.

Hannah opened her mouth to speak into the phone, but Mrs. Wilson cut in first.

"It's all right. I heard that."

There was a pause, long enough for them to look anxiously at each other, wondering if they'd been cut off, before Mrs. Wilson spoke again. Her voice sounded tight and unsteady, as if she was trying to suppress some strong emotion.

"Listen. I've no idea why you want to know all this, but since you do, I'll tell you. Only don't blame me if you wish you'd never asked!"

They waited, Sam's eyes wide with anticipation, Hannah feeling a mixture of excitement and dread. Then the voice began again.

"Two weeks before Maisie died, her mother ran off with a traveling salesman. It was a terrible scandal at the time—in all the newspapers, I believe. The story went that they'd been planning it for months but never told a soul. She left no note—nothing but a pile of debts and a houseful of servants with nothing to live on. But the thing no one could forgive her for was that she left behind her little daughter. She knew Maisie had only a few weeks to live, but she was so taken up with that worthless scoundrel that she left her without even saying good-bye! And in the end, there was scarcely money enough to bury the poor little mite. The servants had to make up the shortfall themselves, and it was hard enough for them as it was." Mrs. Wilson's voice was shaking now. "The worst of it was that Maisie adored her mother. Worshipped the ground she walked on. She'd have done anything to please her, to make her love her in return, but it didn't make any difference. Caroline Holt took less notice of her than if she'd been a stray dog—hardly went near her all the time she was ill. She never cared tuppence for the child!"

There was silence for a few seconds after she'd finished. Then Hannah spoke. "Thank you, Mrs. Wilson. I'm sorry if it's upset you, talking about all this." It was a lame apology, but what else could she say?

"That's all right, dear." The voice seemed calmer now. "It's silly, isn't it? Getting worked up about a tragedy that happened so long ago. But the thought of that little girl going through so much suffering without a word of comfort from the one person in the world she longed to hear it from . . . well, the story has always haunted me. There's something terrible about a mother who doesn't love her child!"

And then Hannah remembered how Mrs. Wilson had said that she and her husband had wanted children but hadn't been able to have any. No wonder she'd been so angry and upset about what had happened to Maisie.

Hannah thanked her again, said good night, and hung up. Sam was looking bleak, and neither of them spoke for a few moments.

"We should have listened to Millie Murdoch," he said gloomily. "When we told her about all the things going on in the house, she said it sounded like attention seeking. That was the clue to it all, just like it was with Henry Knight."

"And even before that, the doll should have warned us something was wrong," muttered Hannah. "Remember how we found it? Just chucked there like a worthless piece of junk! What mother would leave her kid's precious possession to gather dust until some stranger discovered it a hundred and forty years later!"

They sat side by side, silently considering the sad little tale. Then Sam stood up.

"We're forgetting something," he said, sticking his hands in his pockets and shaking his head impatiently. "Millie Murdoch said that the arsenic would have to have been added to a person's food or drink over a long time, didn't she?"

"Yes."

"Well, that lady you spoke to said that Mrs. Holt

never went near Maisie when she was ill. More than that, she doesn't seem to have taken any notice of her at all. In other words, she may have been a lousy mother, but there's no way she could have been our murderer!"

thirty-one

FLYING BIRD

HANNAH LEANED HER ELBOWS on the table and looked again at the photograph, scrutinizing the solemn faces one by one. Then she pushed it away from her, shivering.

"It's cold in here. It may be Midsummer, but right now it doesn't feel like it. This house is damp."

"I forgot to tell you. Rainwater's getting in upstairs. I put a bowl on the landing to catch the drips, but you might want to check your bedroom."

She nodded, but without enthusiasm.

"And while you're doing that, I'll switch on the heater in the other room, and we can sit in there and talk. It'll be more cheerful."

"Okay." She made no move, however, but continued to sit there, her head in her hands.

Sam got up, crossed the hall into the living room, and switched on the electric heater. There was a smell of scorched dust as it warmed up, but the glow was comforting, even if it didn't do much to dispel the damp atmosphere. He was about to leave the room when he noticed Hannah's schoolbag lying on the floor, its contents still scattered where he'd left it after searching for paper and a pencil to play Scrabble. Just in case it caused any awkward questions, he knelt down and began to gather up the books and pens, stuffing them hastily inside the bag. It wasn't until he had finished and stood up that he spied one last item—a piece of paper, much folded and crushed—lying underneath a chair. Bending down to retrieve it, he grinned wryly, recognizing one of his own airplanes. It certainly wasn't going to be doing much flying now! He was about to chuck it in the wastepaper basket when something stopped him. He stared at the crumpled paper. Then, gradually, his heart started to beat a little faster.

Because, of course, to a Victorian child, what he held in his hand wasn't an airplane at all. It was a flying bird.

Hannah hadn't moved from the kitchen table. She sat there, still with her head in her hands. She knew she should go and check on her bedroom but couldn't summon the energy just then. The cold and damp seemed to have seeped into her bones. And she noticed for the first time how quiet the house was. The rain had stopped now, and the only sound in the kitchen was the faint whir coming from the refrigerator.

She had been sitting there, quite still, for about ten minutes, when she heard the noise. An odd, splitting sound was followed a few seconds later by a dull, muffled thump. Frowning, she stood up. The noise had come from directly above her head, which was where her bedroom was. Sam must have gone up there to check on the damage.

"Are you okay?" she called. "Sam?"

When he didn't answer, she went out into the hall, in time to see him coming out of the living room.

"What happened? That sounded like it came from your room. Did you move something in there?" he demanded.

"I haven't been up there! I thought you—" She stopped. They stared at one another, each trying not to see the alarm in the other's eyes.

Sam ran lightly halfway up the staircase. "Who's there?" His voice echoed slightly around the stairwell, then faded into silence. Complete silence.

"The front door was locked when we got back

from the fair. Could anyone have gotten in through a window?"

"I don't know. Should we call the police?" she whispered.

He shook his head and walked slowly and quietly up the remaining stairs. When he reached the landing, he put out his hand to the light switch and pressed it. Nothing happened. "Fetch a flashlight," he muttered.

She ran across the hallway, picked up the heavy flashlight that was kept by the front door, and with legs now feeling like jelly, mounted the stairs.

Sam was kneeling in front of the closed door of her bedroom, trying to look through the keyhole. "It's too dark in there. Can't see a thing." He stood up, took the flashlight from her, and switched it on. Then, drawing a deep breath, he flung open the door.

There was no one there. But a sour, acrid smell hit them at the same moment as the beam of light showed a scene of utter devastation. Above the fireplace, a large section of the ceiling had come down, bringing with it a great swath of waterlogged paper from the chimneypiece. It hung in folds over the mantelpiece, like a huge, sodden curtain.

But that wasn't what made Hannah stare, transfixed in terrified disbelief. It was what lay beneath.

It was a repeated pattern of ash leaves. The long,

pointed spears had faded slightly over the years, but only slightly, and in the clear beam of the flashlight it was possible to see that once they had been a bright, vivid green.

thirty-two

THE VEIL BETWEEN
THE WORLDS

HANNAH HAD NO CLEAR memory of stumbling down-stairs—all she wanted to do was to get out of that horrible room as fast as possible. Back in the living room, she crouched, shivering, in front of the electric heater, her body and brain numb with shock.

Sam knelt beside her, his arm around her shoulders, waiting for the shaking to stop.

After a few minutes she managed to stand up and walk groggily to the sofa, sinking down on the cushions, her head thrown back, eyes closed. Sam joined her but said nothing for now, giving her time to recover.

At last Hannah opened her eyes and looked at him. "Maisie wasn't dreaming at all, was she? She *saw* those leaves. They were all around her on the wallpaper!"

"Didn't I say at the beginning that they could have been *your* dreams, but not necessarily *hers*? Remember what Millie Murdoch told us, that the first symptoms of arsenic poisoning are drowsiness—confusion. If she'd been reading those stories about kids getting lost in a forest, it's easy to see how she could have jumbled everything up so it seemed to her like *she* was in a forest too. Waiting for the wicked witch to appear. And the witch did appear, didn't she? Only it was really her aunt, bringing medicine in a cup. Isn't that what you saw in your dream?"

"I suppose it could have been." With an effort, Hannah sat up, trying to make herself think clearly, logically. "When Maisie was ill, she would have been lying in bed a lot of the time. The sun might have been shining outside. If it shone on the wallpaper, it would have made the leaves sparkle, just like in my dream, but the sky between them wouldn't have been blue, of course, because the wallpaper's background is *white*. That's why I thought it looked overcast."

"And she could have heard the birds singing outside, maybe?"

"Maybe."

"What about the fire? The one you could hear crackling."

Hannah frowned and bit her lip. "Not sure. I

suppose there could have been a bonfire in the garden or something, but it seemed too close for that."

"Just a minute . . . isn't there a fireplace in that room? It's boarded over now, but it could have been lit then, couldn't it? Especially as Maisie was sick."

"Then why couldn't I see it?"

"Her bed was in a different place?"

"But I don't think it was," said Hannah slowly. "There was that little polished table, you see. The one with the cloth and the water pitcher. It was right there—beside me. I'm pretty sure Maisie's bed was exactly where mine is now, only . . . wait! Victorian beds were much higher than ours. My grandmother's got one, and when I was little I always hade to be lifted into it whenever I went to stay. If Maisie had been a couple of feet higher, and lying down, she could have *heard* the fire but not *seen* it. And it explains why the doll's face was so close—she must have had it lying in the bed right next to her!"

"Exactly. You were seeing that room just like it looked to Maisie, *a hundred and forty years ago.*"

Suddenly Hannah collapsed back against the sofa cushions. She had begun to shiver again. "How can we be talking about all this so calmly? It's creepy! And . . . and it still doesn't tell us who murdered Maisie!"

"No? I think it does," he replied quietly. "You'd

better read this." And he handed her a sheet of crumpled paper.

She stared blankly, first at the sheet, then at him. "What is this?"

"Emily's notes on the death of Napoleon. Remember she couldn't find them that day in the library? It's because I'd picked the page up by accident and made an airplane out of it."

At any other time she would have laughed. But not now. "I don't want to read it. Just tell me what you've found out, Sam. Please tell me what Napoleon has to do with all this!"

He sat still for a moment, looking away from her, as if trying to decide how to tackle it, where to begin. Then he turned back.

"Okay. The part about the lock of hair and the analysis you already know. Obviously. But for some reason Emily didn't tell you what happened afterward?"

"No. She didn't."

"Well, it turns out that quite a long time later, a scientist asked a weird question. The question was, what color was Napoleon's wallpaper?"

Hannah's eyes widened, but she said nothing.

"He wanted to know if it had been *green*."

She swallowed. "Go on."

"I'll read the next bit. It'll be simpler." He looked down at the notes, flattening out the creases with the palm of his hand.

"'The answer he received was that the wallpaper in the main room at Longwood on the island of Saint Helena was mostly red but contained elements of green, which he held to be significant on the basis of the following data.'"

Sam glanced up. Hannah was sitting rigidly, her face pale.

"Are you ready for this?"

She nodded.

"Right. Here goes." He took a deep breath and started to read again.

"'Sometime in the late 1700s, a bright-green wallpaper dye had been developed. The color was attractive, it was easy to make, and it soon became very popular. It was called Scheele's Green after the man who invented it. What wasn't generally known was that something called copper arsenite was used in the manufacturing, and it was only when this paper had been in common use for about seventy years that somebody noticed that when it hung in a damp room, it gave off an odd smell. Green was a particularly popular color for bedrooms, and at around this time, it must have occurred to people as odd that so many of these green-papered bedrooms turned into sickrooms and, often, worse. At first, deaths and illnesses attributed to green-papered rooms were thought to be caused by flecks of green dust that detached themselves from the paper and were then breathed in. It wasn't until years later that an Italian chemist worked out that fungi living on wallpaper paste converted inorganic arsenic into a gas, which, in the right conditions, could become lethal.'"

He paused for a few seconds before quietly reading the final sentence.

"'It is now accepted that arsenic gas from wallpaper was responsible for thousands of previously unexplained nineteenth-century deaths, many of them young children, dying in their own green-decorated bedrooms.'"

After he'd finished, they were both silent for some time. Hannah realized that all the time he'd been reading, her muscles had been locked in tension. Now she released them and found she was shaking again.

"Hey! You okay?" He looked at her in concern. "Why don't you move closer to the fire? I'll get something to put over you."

She submitted to being moved into a chair nearer the fire while he fetched his jacket from the hall and tucked it in around her. It smelled comfortingly of him, but she still felt weak from this new shock. "It was the *wallpaper* that killed her!" she said huskily.

He nodded. "No wonder those green leaves gave you nightmares. They were deadly!"

Again they said nothing for a little while, each considering the implications of what they'd just learned, in a silence broken only by the soft ticking of the grandfather clock.

At last, warmed by the fire, Hannah stopped shaking. Gradually her color began to return.

"You know, I think I've figured out what might have caused the dreams. I never made the connection before, but now, looking back, I never had them when the weather was dry. *Only when it was very damp.* And those are exactly the conditions that would have made the paper lethal! Remember that weird smell in the room? I've noticed it before, just after waking from a nightmare."

"You think the poison is still active?" He looked at her in alarm.

She shook her head. "After all this time? But what if something in the atmosphere triggered a kind of memory in the room?"

"And your brain connected with that memory while you were asleep?"

Hannah didn't reply straightaway. She was

recalling the words of the woman in the shop.

"People always seem to move out after a spell of wet weather."

Then something else came back to her. Something Miss Murdoch had said once, at Halloween.

"Remember, on this night the veil between the worlds is at its thinnest!"

The past was like this house—concealed by layer upon layer of more recent history, but never entirely eradicated. Could it be that at certain times of year, given the right conditions, it might be possible to glimpse beyond those layers to the things that lurked beneath? Had other people seen strange things at this time of year? Things they couldn't handle?

She sighed. "I don't know what was happening in *my* brain, but I wonder what was going on in Laetitia's. Mrs. Grocott said she was a clever woman. D'you think she had an idea Maisie was being poisoned? Was that why she insisted on taking over all the nursing— trying to get Maisie moved to her own room? We were so busy suspecting *her* that we never thought about it the other way around. What if *she* suspected the *servants*? No wonder they didn't like her. She probably acted like she didn't trust them, and showed it!"

"And then when Maisie got worse, which she was bound to do—being in that room—it would have given them even more reason to suspect *her*. Add to that the bruises and the state of the doll, and . . ."

Sam stopped. They stared at each other in horror as the significance of what he'd just said dawned on them both at the same time.

"If Maisie wasn't murdered by anyone in this house," Hannah whispered, *"then who stuck the pins into that doll?"*

thirty-three

MAISIE'S SECRET

The QUESTION CAME LIKE a dousing of cold water, for a moment threatening to wash away their carefully constructed theory as if it were a sand castle about to be toppled by the advancing tide.

Hannah forced herself to think of that monstrous creature, which, even after more than a hundred years, still had had the stench of evil clinging to it. She saw again those wild, staring eyes, the disfiguring brown stains on the body, the white dress that had been a copy of Maisie's own. And then she remembered something her mother had said on first seeing that dress. Something that had seemed trivial at the time.

"These holes are way too big for the buttons. That's unusual. Victorian sewing is usually so neat."

What did that mean? That the doll's dress had been changed by somebody who wasn't very good at sewing? Or by someone who was just learning how to sew? Like a child, for example. A child who had carefully embroidered a handkerchief for her mother.

Again she heard her own mother's words.

"I suspect she had a certain amount of help with this. It's pretty impressive for a nine-year-old!"

Of course. Her aunt would have helped her to sew the handkerchief, patiently showing her the stitches, correcting her when she went wrong. But the doll had been different. That had been altered in secret. She had had no help there.

And finally Hannah thought of Laetitia, who, with selfless devotion, had carefully concealed those little treasures so that Maisie would never find them and know that her mother hadn't wanted them. But it wasn't Laetitia's love that Maisie had needed. So she had rejected it, thrown it back, like the cup in her dream, with all the careless cruelty of childhood suffering, and set about her diabolical little scheme.

Now that they knew all the rest, it was so obvious.

"It was Maisie," she said, shivering. "Maisie did it!"

Sam said nothing, but she could see from his face that he knew she was right.

One by one, all the layers of deception and

misconstruction were being stripped away, leaving only the stark, dismal truth. The story might be old and forgotten, but like the hidden paper, it had always been there.

"There's just one thing," he said wearily. "It's not important, and I don't suppose we're ever going to find out now, but . . . those bruises on the doll. If Maisie wanted to make them look like her own bruises, why didn't she try to make them more realistic—more random?"

And now at last, ridiculously, Hannah found herself close to tears. "I forgot! Inspector Bean told me what they were, but I didn't bother about it at the time because I was only thinking about the hair. Those brown marks on the body weren't ever supposed to be bruises. They're iodine. Maisie must have taken the pins out when she realized her mother wasn't taking any notice of them, but the holes they left showed her that she'd been unkind to her doll, and she wanted to make it better. Iodine's an antiseptic. You see," she whispered, trying to control her trembling voice, "she was only a *little* girl."

Sam looked at her somberly for a few moments, then got up and left the room. He returned a few seconds later with a paper towel. "Here."

"Thanks." She took it and blew her nose.

"You know," he said, sitting down next to her on the sofa, "I have a feeling that you were meant to find those things—the doll, the box, the paints, the book of fairy tales. Without them, you couldn't make sense of what the house was trying to tell you."

"You think it was this *house* that was trying to tell me? Why not Maisie? And come to that, why not *us*? We've solved this together, haven't we?"

"The house helped us uncover the *story*," he said slowly. "That's always been there, waiting for someone who'd take enough trouble to find out the truth. But . . ." He hesitated, not wanting to burden her with more than she could take just then. "I think that the *messages* were from Maisie herself, and they were meant for you."

Hannah looked bleakly at him. Then she rubbed her eyes. "You may be right, but . . . I'm sorry, I can't think about it anymore tonight."

Sam got up and walked to the window, drawing the curtain aside a little. "The sky's cleared. It's a fine night." He looked at his watch. "And it's almost one a.m. We may as well try and get some sleep."

They both knew that sleeping on the upper floor was out of the question that night. Instead, Hannah fetched a spare blanket from the linen closet and they lay down on the sofa, foot to foot. Soon she heard

Sam's quiet snoring.

But in spite of her exhaustion, Hannah couldn't sleep. She heard the clock strike two, then three. Sometime between four and five, a thin light began to creep around the edges of the drawn curtains, and not long after that the birds started singing. She lay there, listening to them, watching the light gradually change from pale to gold as the new day dawned.

At last she gave up, slid off the sofa, and padded to the window. Pulling the curtain aside a few inches, she looked out. The climbing sun had now turned the sky from gold to a soft, shimmering turquoise, and the leaves, still wet from last night's rain, shone like bright jewels. She opened the window and leaned out, breathing the cool, fresh air. She stayed there for a few minutes; then a faint sound made her turn her head. She listened. It was a very soft tapping noise. Puzzled, she closed the window, crossed the room, and went into the hall, but the tapping had stopped now. She opened the front door and looked out. Nobody was there.

And then she heard it again, a little louder this time. A gentle but insistent knocking, coming, she now realized, not from the front but from the back of the house.

She frowned. Had Mom forgotten to take a key

with her, and was she back now, trying to get in?

Leaving the front door on the latch, Hannah opened the little gate at the side of the house and stepped through. The overgrown lawn, drenched by the storm, looked even more neglected now, but that wasn't what made Hannah blink suddenly in surprise. It was the bench. She had come around the side of the house now and could see it clearly. There was something lying on the wooden slats. Something white and rectangular. Drawing closer, she could see now that it was her sketch pad, with a pencil lying neatly beside it. She stared in astonishment. Why was it here? If it had been out all night, it would be ruined. Slowly she walked toward the bench. But when she reached it and picked up the sketch pad, she found that it was quite dry. It must have been put there since last night. But by whom? She was about to take it back inside when something made her turn toward the house.

Just below the steps, in front of the tall windows, stood a little girl in a long white dress with a frilled hem and a blue sash.

thirty-four

DRAWING OUT

BUT THE BRIGHT, SMILING confidence of that long-ago September day was all gone now. Instead, Maisie stood with her hands clasped in front of her and her head bent submissively, in the attitude of a penitent.

Later, looking back on that moment, Hannah could never quite explain to herself why she had felt no fear. It was as though, in the soft dawn of the Midsummer morning, within the shadow of the old house, she knew instinctively that no harm could come to either of them. The story was nearly over. The wicked witches, the bad fairies, the evil stepmothers had vanished with the night, and now all that remained was for her was to provide a happy ending. So she sat down on the bench, picked up the sketchbook, and began to draw.

The lines flowed easily, just as they had once before, but this time it was as though the house, in providing the background, were giving its blessing to a child who had suffered so much and in turn caused suffering within its walls. The sketch took perhaps ten minutes, and when Hannah had finished, she knew that it was a true likeness, for the truth was told now, and would never need telling again. When she at last laid the book aside and looked up, Maisie wasn't there anymore.

If there had been any lingering doubt in her mind, it evaporated the moment she opened the front door of Cowleigh Lodge and stepped into the hall. The atmosphere hadn't changed so much as disappeared. Those walls had nothing to hide—the rooms held no dark secrets. It was simply a house, badly in need of repair.

There was just one more thing to do. Running lightly up the stairs, she pushed open the door of her bedroom, stepped inside, and forced herself to look once more at the deadly ash leaves. But now the pattern looked only forlorn, shabby, its terror faded in the early-morning light, like the memory of a bad dream. Looking away at last, she leafed through her sketchbook until she found the first drawing of Maisie—the one that had started it all. Skirting the chaos on the floor, she walked over to the dressing table, took the calendar page from the mirror, and holding it together with the drawing, tore them both into tiny shreds. Then she walked over to the window and scattered the pieces on the grass below. The rain and the wind would do the rest.

Down in the living room, Sam was still dead to the world and snoring lightly. For a moment she considered waking him to tell him what had happened, but then decided to wait. There was no hurry. Yawning, she lay down on the sofa, and just before falling asleep, she noticed that Toby was back on the hearth rug.

She woke just before eleven, to the smell of coffee and frying bacon and the sound of voices coming from the kitchen. Her mother must have returned and was chatting with Sam. For a few moments Hannah lay there drowsily, listening to them. Then she sat up. Surely she could hear more than just two people? There was someone else there with them. Someone whose voice was just as familiar but . . . it couldn't be. Could it? She got up, padded across the hall, and stuck her head through the kitchen doorway.

And there was her father, calmly seated at the kitchen table opposite Sam and her mother, sipping coffee just as if he'd never been away.

"Dad!"

Mr. Price hastily put down his cup just as a delighted Hannah hurled herself on him. He grinned and hugged her. "Hello, Sleeping Beauty. How are you?"

"How long have you been here?" she demanded. "Why are you back now? And why didn't you wake me sooner?"

"To answer in order," he replied, smiling and gently pushing her into a chair, "we got back about an hour ago, the person I was standing in for recovered in time to take over the last week of the tour, and we didn't wake you because Sam said you'd had a bad night."

"Did you know about this, Mom? Is that why you—"

"Certainly not!" protested her mother. "I'd only just left your aunt's house when I got a call to say that Dad was at the airport. He hadn't let us know beforehand, just in case the flight was delayed or canceled at the last minute. It was sheer chance that I happened to be near enough to pick him up."

Hannah stopped asking questions and watched contentedly as her mother laid a plateful of eggs and bacon in front of her. She suddenly felt ravenous. As she tucked in, Dad started to tell them about his trip, interrupted from time to time by his wife asking if all American women really were beautifully dressed and groomed all the time and Sam wanting to know if it was true that the policemen invariably brandished guns and were prepared to shoot on sight. Both seemed disappointed to discover that the country wasn't all they'd been led to believe from the movies.

"And now," said Dad, "perhaps you'd care to tell me what you and your mother have been doing to this house? I leave you on your own for a month and get back to a wreck!" His tone was joking, but there was genuine puzzlement in his eyes.

Hannah looked at Sam, who shrugged and turned to Mrs. Price. She smiled nervously and got up to refill the coffeepot.

Mr. Price noted the evasion, but he didn't pursue it just then. Instead he cleared his throat and said, "Oh, well, I don't suppose it matters much, because we'll only be here for a couple more days."

"What?" Hannah paused in the act of helping herself to more eggs and bacon.

"I was telling your mother in the car. Apparently our house wasn't in quite such a dire state as that surveyor seemed to think. It didn't need underpinning—only reinforcing. The work was finished last week, and we can move back as soon as we like."

"You mean we're going home?"

"Of course. What is there to keep us here?"

It wasn't meant to be a question, but the house, if not her father, seemed to require an answer. "Nothing," she said softly. "Nothing at all."

Sam looked at her. Then he laid down his knife and fork, glanced casually at his watch, and stood up. "I'd better be going. You'll have stuff to talk about."

Hannah followed him to the hall, closing the kitchen door behind them. When they reached the front door, he paused. "It's all over, isn't it? Maisie . . . she's gone?"

Despite the upward inflection of his voice, this wasn't a question either, and Hannah knew it.

"Yes. She's gone."

"Are you going to tell me how?"

"Remember you said that this all started because I'd drawn her into my life?"

He nodded.

"Well, this morning, I drew her out."

She waited for him to ask more, but, oddly, he didn't. It was as if, on that magical morning, he, like her, understood that some things were better not explained but simply accepted, and that having accompanied her on her journey toward the truth, his part in the story had ended. The final pages had always been meant for her alone.

"See you, then." He grinned and left.

Later that day, while Mom prepared a special celebratory evening meal in the kitchen, Hannah found herself alone with her father in the living room.

"D'you want to sit down for a moment?" Dad pointed to a chair, and Hannah noticed that he was holding what looked like a copy of their rental agreement.

She lowered herself anxiously onto the edge of the seat. "I suppose you're worried about all the damage. Will they make us pay for redecorating?"

Her father drummed his fingers thoughtfully on the arm of his chair, and Hannah began to think he hadn't heard her.

"Dad?"

"Yes?"

"I said, will we have to pay for the damage to the house?"

"What? Oh. No. I shouldn't imagine so. Tell me . . ." His voice was casual. "Have you been okay here? No, um, problems?"

"Other than all this?" She waved a hand to indicate the sorry state of the house.

"Other than all that."

Hannah decided to lie. Under the circumstances, it seemed not only the simplest but the kindest thing to do. "No problems," she said, crossing her fingers and smiling brightly. "Why do you ask?"

He frowned. "Only that, from my point of view, there's something rather odd."

"Oh? What?"

"Well, I found this place through an ad in the local paper, as you may remember."

"Yes."

"And you may also remember your mother saying that the rent seemed very low for a house in this neighborhood?"

"Yes." Hannah began to feel uneasy. "Was there some mistake? Are we going to have to pay a lot more?"

"Not exactly. You see, when Mom called me to say she was worried about the way the house seemed to be deteriorating, I called the real estate agency."

"And?"

"Not only did they not know who I was, they had absolutely no record of any agreement to rent this house at all. According to them, the place is uninhabitable owing to the state of the roof."

Dad looked straight at her now, and Hannah felt a prickling sensation at the base of her spine. "But . . . you got the key, with that letter." She pointed to the document on the arm of the chair. "If the agency didn't send them, then who did?"

"That's just what they'd like to know. It's odd, isn't it? If it didn't seem so utterly impossible, I'd almost have said that it wasn't so much that we found this house as that the house found *us*. What do you think?"

But Hannah was saved from having to say what she thought by the appearance of her mother, telling them that dinner was ready.

There was just one other unusual occurrence that day, and this was witnessed by the two Misses Pettifer, who, returning rather later than usual from an evening playing string quartets at the house of a friend, decided to take a shortcut across John's Field.

The fair was winding down now, but there were still one or two people about, and as they passed the bumper cars, the loud, brash music made them wince and quicken their step.

Then, suddenly, one of them stopped and stared. Two cars were hurtling wildly around the ring, their occupants shouting and hooting in glee.

"What is the matter, Dorothy?" asked her sister impatiently. "Do come along!"

Reluctantly Dorothy turned away and continued walking, but every so often she glanced back. "Did you see them, Hilda?"

"Who?"

"Those two people in the cars. A young boy with red hair, and a . . . a rather large man." She giggled nervously. "Just for a moment, I could have sworn that the man was none other than our dear bishop!"

"Don't be absurd," said Hilda sternly. "You know perfectly well you need new glasses."

Nevertheless, when her sister wasn't looking, Hilda stole a quick glance at the brightly lit ring and blinked. Twice. "Impossible," she muttered to herself, and shook her head. "It's these long evenings making the light play tricks." Determinedly squaring her shoulders, she walked on.

In her opinion, it was a thoroughly odd time of year.

ACKNOWLEDGMENTS

I WOULD LIKE TO THANK the folowing people who assisted with the writing of this little ghost story: Sarah Shumway and Katherine Tegen for their sensitive, thorough, and thoughtful editing; my agent Eunice McMullen for her patience in listening to my frequent worries; and my partner, Gordon, and his friends Sally, Shuna, and Carol, who offered support and helpful suggestions. Also Gwen Fisher for advice with American idiom. Most of all, thanks to my daughter Louisa, who painstakingly read every draft and kept me sane. Well, almost.